The Turquoise Trader
A Zia Yazzie Novel

PATRICIA BEZUNARTEA

Cover design, electronic book design and author photo by Heather J. Kirk, PhotoGraphic Artistry and Publishing, Scottsdale, AZ

For additional information please contact:

pat@patriciabezunartea.com
www.patriciabezunartea.com
www.theturquoisetrader.com

Bezunartea, Patricia
The Turquoise Trader: A Zia Yazzie Novel

     1.Southwestern
     2.Native American
     3.Romance
     4.Business

ISBN-13: 978-0692412732
ISBN-10: 0692412735

DEDICATION

Dedicated to the loving memory of my late husband, Frank Bezunartea, who made this book possible, and to the inspiration of my son, Zack Bezunartea, and daughter, Amy Bezunartea.

Great thanks and appreciation to Deborah Hilcove of BelVista Publishers, for her expert editing, friendship and writing partnership.

Special thanks to Mike Sweeney, who shares my life and honors my love of writing.

.

CONTENTS

PART 1: THE WINDS OF CHANGE

December 29, 1973

The Indian jewelry craze hit a fever pitch in Gallup, New Mexico, and Ben Monroe stood to make a bundle of money. But he needed help. It was pay-back time, and he was calling in a debt—it was personal, private and secret.

***

Unlatching the east-facing hogan door, Zia Yazzie stepped into the icy stillness and met the late December dawn. The crisp air held the scent of piñon smoke from the wood stove, and the sky was heavy with snow clouds. He glanced north where piñon and juniper grew sturdy against the shadow of the red sandstone cliffs. To the east he could barely picture the outline of Mt. Taylor—Turquoise Mountain—one of the four sacred mountains of his Navajo people.

He slipped the soft leather pollen pouch from his pocket, untied the thin lanyard and took a pinch of corn pollen between his thumb and forefinger. After he sprinkled the pollen on his tongue, he touched the top of his head and then scattered the remaining flecks into the morning breeze as an offering to the Holy Deities.

He stepped back inside the small eight-sided dwelling and walked clockwise toward the warmth of the wood stove, where his mother stood tossing coffee grounds into the water boiling away in the blue speckled enamelware coffee pot. A few minutes later they sat together at a small table to capture the warmth and enjoy their coffee.

"It's nice to have you home from Albuquerque, Son. You have almost a month before your final semester of college." She placed her hand on her heart. "The first in our clan to graduate from college…you make me proud."

"Everything seems to be falling into place for me, Mother," he smiled. "All those nights of studying by flashlight here in our hogan have paid off."

"Speaking of paid off, Son, you have your father to thank for paying your tuition."

He put his head down. "Yes, he's always supported me financially... but... I feel like you gave up your life because of me."

Anjelah Yazzie stared in disbelief.

"Zia, you are my blessing from the Creator. Never should you think that."

They each turned with a start at the sound of an approaching car, its tires crunching along the dirt road.

Zia opened the door to see the dark blue Lincoln town car parking in front of the hogan. When Anjelah saw Ben Monroe hop out of the car, she straightened her velveteen blouse, ruffled her calico skirt into place and smoothed her thick, black hair which was softly wound into a knot and held with a domed silver barrette.

Zia studied her delicate features, looking for any sign that she cared for Ben Monroe.

Zia watched him toss a cigarette into the dirt as he strode toward the hogan. In jeans, cowboy shirt, snakeskin boots and leather jacket, he looked the part of a rich Gallup Indian arts and crafts dealer— wearing his trademark Robert Leekya watch-bracelet and ring, set with stunning large turquoise nuggets.

Zia never failed to notice their strong resemblance—in appearance—nothing else.

I'm Navajo. It seems bizarre that this White man is actually my father, he thought.

Ben stood in the doorway to observe the customary moment of silence that signified prayer upon entering a hogan. Then he automatically walked clockwise— Navajo tradition—toward the wood stove in the center of the dwelling.

"Long time no look," Ben clipped, mimicking a Navajo accent. But that's what he always said when he showed up—which was rarely.

"Angie, how've you been?" he said, leaning over to give her a peck on the cheek.

Before she could answer, he reached out and gave Zia a hearty handshake. The handshake was not a Navajo custom, but Ben had taught Zia the importance of shaking hands in the outside world.

Zia felt sorry for his mother.

Anjelah stepped to the wood stove and poured strong black coffee into another enamelware mug for Ben and refilled theirs.

Ben stood sipping his coffee and began to pace and looked from Anjelah to Zia. They sat quietly waiting for him to talk about his favorite subjects—business and money.

He raked his fingers through his dark hair and paced the floor with his gaze focused on Zia.

"This Indian jewelry boom is tremendous, Zia. It's an opportunity to make a lot more money, and I need your help. I need someone I can trust...someone I can teach the business. You're old enough now...so it has to be you."

Zia froze. A sick feeling locked the pit of his stomach. What was his father suggesting? Was this some kind of a trap?

He glanced at his mother, knowing how much his education meant to her, but she remained silent.

"What about college? I'll graduate in May."

"College? That won't help you make money," Ben said, turning to set his cup down for Anjelah to pour more coffee. *Now* is the time to make money."

Ben blew on the hot coffee and sipped it slowly.

"Ants. Ants. College just makes people into trails of ants. You have to know *how* to make money. They can't teach you that in college. But I can teach you."

Zia cringed.

"But, my plans..." Zia stopped and turned away. He didn't dare bring up his dreams of changing education on the reservation—that would have been met with pure disdain by his father.

His heartbeat quickened. He took a deep breath and looked toward his mother for a way out, but she sat with her head down, wringing her hands. It was obvious she knew her place.

Why me, Zia thought as he paced, hands in his pockets—staring at the floor. Didn't his father have a son or daughter from his "real" family who was old enough? But he knew nothing of Ben's other life. Besides, Zia had been a secret for 21 years—why bring him around now?

Before Zia could greet the next sunrise on the reservation, he was whisked away to Gallup and delivered to a studio apartment that Ben kept in downtown. He awakened to a gray dawn that revealed old brick buildings from the town's coal and railroad era—the town now considered "The Indian Capital of the World."

His felt like his well-planned life was evaporating. Why didn't he stand up for himself? What weird sense of duty made him go along with his father's plans? He decided he would have to make the best of it—determined it wouldn't last. Closing the blinds, he cut off the dim sunrise and stepped outside into his new life.

The winds of change blew against him, and snow clouds matched his mood—low and heavy like they might suffocate him as he walked toward Route 66. He zipped his wool jacket, flipped the collar up around his neck and slipped his hands into the pockets of his worn Wranglers. When he reached the corner of Coal and Fifth Street, he spotted Boyd's Café—"Breakfast from 6:00 a.m." He opened the door of the '50s era diner, and a bell sounded his arrival.

The Navajo waitress greeted him, grabbed a menu and seated him at one of the Formica-topped booths—where the lumpy seats were upholstered in red Naugahyde. Without asking, she automatically poured him a cup of coffee.

He ordered *atole*. The blue cornmeal mush reminded him of home. He stirred in a little brown sugar and warmed milk—just the way he liked it. But, the atole couldn't feed his spirit—he was out-of-place.

Zia paid his check from the advance Ben had given him the day before. He stepped outside, then turned and walked north alongside Boyd's toward Route 66 and the trading post, where he was scheduled to meet his father before the other employees arrived. The railroad tracks ran parallel to the highway, and a loud whistle and deadening rumble announced the train's arrival as the freight cars whizzed past.

By the time he reached the store, a hint of sunshine peeked through the snow clouds. Remains of the previous night—empty and broken Roma and Thunderbird wine bottles glistened along the sidewalk. He knew drunken Navajos had huddled in the doorways the night before—passed-out—until they were picked up and either jailed or housed for the night so they wouldn't freeze to death, awaiting another forgiving sunrise.

Alcoholism is the scourge of my people, he thought, picking up paper bags and wine bottles from the store's entrance and waiting for his father. Ben had said he wanted to meet Zia early—before any of the other employees arrived.

Zia stepped back and looked up at the painted wooden sign—Monroe Trading Company.

"Good morning, Zia." Ben seemed happy to see him, patting him on the back. As Ben dug for his keys, the first fat snowflakes began to fall. It would be a wet snow Zia thought. It's when the flakes came down in small beads that the storm lasts and drops a foot or more of fluffy white powder. His grandmother had taught him that when he was a child.

After Ben unlocked the door and hit the lights, Zia stepped into the store with its dazzling array of showcases filled with Indian jewelry—walls covered with Navajo rugs and paintings and shelves lined with Pueblo pottery and Hopi kachinas. He walked across the wood plank floor and took it all in. The large rectangular haven of merchandise even had a glass-enclosed office in the far corner next to a large vault. All he could say was, "Wow."

A proud grin spread across Ben's face.

Zia stood solid, digesting his new environment. Funny, he

thought, under different circumstances, I would probably never go into a store like this.

"Zia, I want to teach you everything about the business," Ben began. "You already know the merchandise…from being around it your whole life. Your family is full of silversmiths and rug weavers—but the business side is different. It's exciting…now more than ever. I'll teach you how to buy, the markups to use and the structures for selling jobber, wholesale and retail."

Zia nodded with fake enthusiasm.

"And I want you to be my mole. No one will know you are my son. I want you to call me Ben."

Oh great, Zia thought, he wants a secret-son spy. What's going on?

"What am I watching for…Ben?"

"Maybe nothing," Ben said. "But keep your eyes and ears open."

Ben slapped him on the back. "Let's get started."

Ben headed to the vault door and twirled through the lock's combination, opening the heavy door in seconds. Inside, a sea of silver and turquoise jewelry met Zia's gaze. It looked like mass production had set in on the reservation.

"This is supply and demand at work, Zia. It's our turn to make the big money."

"Let me show you." Ben detailed his pricing and profit structure, and soon Zia's head was spinning. This was all new to him, and he didn't like it one bit. Those mark-ups and profits…it's downright embarrassing, he thought.

Ben noticed Zia's disapproval.

"Hey, kid, this is nothing, you should see the diamond dealers' markups. Welcome to the real world. And don't think this is all profit. Look around at all the costs—the building, improvements, fixtures, equipment, supplies, utilities, salaries, and on and on. Or like my dad always said, you even have to figure the cost of toilet paper and shoe polish. And don't forget, silver is almost $5.00 an ounce."

He told Zia that he had to learn what sells—from the ordinary to the collectible—what to buy and how much to pay. "If you don't build in enough profit, you're out of business."

By the end of his first day, Zia was numb. That night he dreamed of hundred-dollar-bills rolled up and shooting out of squash blossom necklaces. More bills became arrows—stabbing his bare skin, drawing fresh blood.

***

Greeting the sunrise and Boyd's quickly became Zia's morning routine. When he walked into the diner, the aromas of freshly brewing coffee, frying bacon and tortillas scorching on the grill welcomed him.

"*Ya'at'eeh*," said Betty—her traditional Navajo hello proclaimed the spirit of good. She poured his coffee before he picked up the counter copy of *The Albuquerque Journal*.

Zia sipped coffee and tried to think of a way to complete his final semester at UNM. He planned to call his counselor as soon as he got to the store and set up an appointment. There were still a few weeks before the new semester started—maybe, just maybe, there was a solution.

Besides school, he had a life in Albuquerque, but his friends and roommates didn't know about his dilemma yet. He would have to tell them he was moving, and then pack his books and few belongings.

This feels like the bitter end of my existence, he thought.

Zia was getting to know Ben Monroe better and learning the business. Zia called him Ben, and no one was told he was his son— he was just part of the crew at Monroe Trading Company.

Taking his usual path to the store, he rounded the corner and strolled past Richardson's, staring into the windows of the authentic old trading post. It looked like a museum with old saddles hanging everywhere and pawn jewelry spread against the wall behind showcases. He would love to see inside *their* vault, he thought. He pulled the keys from his pocket, then gathered the empty wine bottles and unlocked the door to open for business.

He scanned the length of showcases of silver and turquoise jewelry, checked the stacks of Navajo rugs and made sure that one or two remained unfolded and dropped on the floor. Ben said if the rugs were too neatly stacked, people were afraid to go through them. He tossed two banded rugs on the floor—like those his grandmother wove. It was a common weaving style, known for its alternating stripes and horizontal bands of geometric designs.

Next, he glanced at the shelves of pottery and kachinas—well merchandised, colorful and attractive. But jewelry was the big seller—jewelry filled the rough-hewn showcases. The bottom level, lined with black velvet, held displays of squash blossoms, wide cuff bracelets and collectible sets. The glass shelves just above that array displayed rows of bracelets, pendants, earrings and rings.

Zia walked toward the vault.

Louise came in quietly, carrying her lunch and thermos as usual, and opened the door to the small office where she did the bookkeeping and bank deposits. She had worked for Ben for many years. She was plump, plain and matronly, and she did her job and minded her own business.

Next Jerry sauntered in, tall, thin with perfect posture—a guy in his 30s who used to sell for a fine jewelry store in San Antonio. He dressed well and sported perfectly-sculpted brown hair. He puffed the last of his cigarette, then flicked it out the door and onto the sidewalk. He turned on the radio and danced across the floor to the country beat as he took off his leather jacket.

"Hey, buddy, what's happenin' this mornin'?"

"Not much, Jerry," Zia commented casually, while concentrating on the vault combination. When he opened the door, he noticed rows of brown paper sacks on the work table in the center of the large vault—each filled with jewelry Ben must have bought last night. Some figures were scratched out with black marker and replaced with quantities and prices written in Ben's handwriting just below. They would have to mark those retail prices on the jewelry with their indelible-ink pens and get it merchandised.

He took the blue bank bag from its usual place on the shelf and strolled to the cash register—turned the key—hit the button to open the drawer and pulled out $200 for the cash drawer. He placed the ones, fives, tens and twenties neatly in their slots facing the same direction. Ben loved his money, and he wanted it orderly. Then Zia took the cash bag with the   lengthy z-tape of yesterday's sales and the fat stack of cash, checks and credit card receipts to Louise. He glanced at the total. Business was good.

Ben was right. They were selling jewelry like wild—especially wholesale. Indian jewelry was the rage—in style—in vogue. Even *The Wall Street Journal* had said it was a good investment. Movie stars were pictured in magazines wearing squash blossom necklaces and concho belts. Lots of other people were trying to cash in on the trend, too— some gas stations had jewelry cases full of silver and turquoise; wives of doctors and lawyers were having jewelry parties; hippies with questionable cash bought Indian jewelry to sell to their friends. Indian jewelry stores were popping up everywhere. Ben Monroe was working non-stop—buying and selling—like a turquoise tornado.

By the time Zia returned from the office, Karen had hurried in and plopped her purse and her ever-present can of Tab on the shelf below the register and slipped out of her fake-fur coat, rolled it up and shoved it into a corner in the vault. She wore a tight-fitting red bell-bottomed jump suit with high-heeled boots. A large silver concho belt hugged her slender hips just below the waist, and the outfit was unzipped enough at the top to reveal her cleavage. Her long blond hair fell in layers of fluffy curls, and her makeup gave her the look of a country-western star—but her Jungle Gardenia perfume was overwhelming.

"Well, well, missy. Look who *earned* her concho belt."

"Shut up, Jerry. Mind your own damn business," Karen snapped.

"Yeah, well my business is to find a way out of this dump of a town, Miss Priss."

"Yeah, please do…and take that chip on your shoulder to a new location."

"Up yours, Karen."

"Well, good riddance to bad rubbish." Karen grabbed the glass cleaner and a few paper towels and cleaned the fingerprints off the showcases.

"What about you, Zia?" Karen looked up from the showcase. "Have something to say about my concho belt?"

"No. I'm Navajo," he switched to his clipped accent. "We don't talk all the time like White people—only say what's necessary."

Zia turned and walked toward the vault. He had heard the gossip about Ben and Karen's affair, and though it offended him, he pushed it out of his thoughts. He just wanted to get along with everyone, do the best job he could, and get this stint over with as soon as possible.

In the meantime, he had a lot to learn about the artisans and the turquoise mines, and he had to become a storehouse of information, even though he had no intention of making a career of the Indian jewelry trade.

He showed the customers how Zuni work was defined by stone-cutting for inlay, cluster and petit-point—and Hopi by overlays of silver with pueblo designs. The strength of silver, chiseled, stamped and set with turquoise stones made Navajo work distinctive.

Ben strolled in the door and behind the showcases to where Zia studied the turquoise map. Zia wanted to do a better job of identifying the turquoise from the mines mostly in Arizona, Nevada, Colorado and parts of Asia.

"Buyers want information," Ben said, pointing into the showcase. This is Morenci turquoise. You can tell by the copper matrix running through the stone. Now look at the Number 8 Spider Web—it's a deeper blue with almost black matrix in thin lines, like spider webbing. Oh… and here's my favorite, Bisbee blue—just look at the depth of color in that stone."

"Ben," Zia put his hands in his pockets, "To Navajos, turquoise is the blue gem of the earth that symbolizes the power of sky and water. Do customers want to know that, too?"

"Absolutely. That's part of the mystique."

Zia understood that turquoise was a by-product of copper and created by water flowing through the copper-laden rock, but rumor had it that a lot of the really good turquoise was being used up fast in the Indian jewelry frenzy and asked Ben about it.

"Some suppliers have started to stabilize the lower quality turquoise," Ben said. "It's more porous, so they use a resin that hardens and seals the stone and enhances the color. I'm not sure how I feel about that, but it's an outcome of necessity, I guess."

Every day, Zia trudged through more information. When the store was quiet, he sat and read the books Ben had accumulated, trying to memorize everything he could so he would appear more professional with the buyers. Information made the jewelry more appealing and desirable—it wasn't just merchandise—and he admitted that buyers liked dealing with him because he was Navajo.

***

The following morning at Boyd's, Zia sipped coffee and thumbed through the paper for the sports section to see the score of the Lobo-Aggie basketball game. It was the state rivalry—University of New Mexico Lobos against New Mexico State Aggies, and this game would advance one of the teams into the next step in the annual NCAA competition.

The Arabs probably took the sports section, he thought, looking back at the group in the last booth. He had heard they bet on a lot of the games—quite the gamblers. He recognized two of them from the store where they often sold jewelry to Ben. They were having a lively discussion in their native tongue—hands flying in the air, engulfed in clouds of cigarette smoke. Zia understood that they had come to the Gallup area many years earlier, selling tapestries on the reservation. Then they traded with the Navajos and Zunis for jewelry and other crafts and sold to dealers and traders, like his father.

Ben told Zia that Gallup had always been an immigrant town, a place where many Greek, Italian and Slavic people had struggled to make a new life in the coal and railroad era and had stayed on for generations. So, it seemed natural that "The Arabs" were accepted.

It was that morning at Boyd's that Zia first saw the pretty girl as she breezed through the café door. She looked like she had just rolled

15

out of bed—but fresh and beautiful. Her long black hair was pulled back in a ponytail, and she wore jeans, a UNM sweatshirt and a down jacket. She gave a big smile and hello to Betty and sat in a booth adjacent to Zia—facing him—and when he looked at her, he suddenly felt awkward trying to swallow the atole.

Zia pretended to read the paper and listened as Betty approached her table.

"Selene, long time no look," she said in her clipped Navajo accent. "What are you doing at home?"

"It's semester break. I have a few weeks until classes start again," Selene said. "How are you, Betty?"

"Pretty good, real fine."

"I don't need a menu, Betty. My green chile alarm clock told me to get over to Boyd's."

Betty chuckled.

Selene rubbed her hands together. "Yes, Betty, I need huevos rancheros with green chile, frijoles and tortillas...you know, *chamuscado*, that extra-scorched way that I like them."

"Got it," Betty said, and gave the cook instructions to nearly burn the tortillas.

Zia smiled to himself.

When her breakfast arrived, Selene savored every bite—and Zia enjoyed watching her.

Soon, a tall fashionably dressed Arab glided through the door. He noticed Selene and as he walked by, he immediately turned to her table. He leaned over close to her and spoke with a familiar Arab accent. "I swear to God, you are more beautiful than ever. If I did not respect your father so much, I would have you."

She looked away as he proceeded to join the group at the back table, the heels of his fancy leather shoes clicking against the worn tile.

"Give me Selene's check please," he motioned to Betty, displaying a large ruby ring and heavy gold watch on his left hand. His strong cologne scent lingered.

Selene's glance met Zia's for an instant. Knowing he had heard the remarks, she rolled her eyes and shrugged her shoulders and gave him a quick self-conscious smile. It was obvious to Zia that she was uncomfortable with the encounter.

He glanced past her out the window, and the angle of the sun told him it was time to leave.

Self-consciously, Zia got up from his booth, and hard as he could try, couldn't think of a thing to say to Selene, but caught her glance again and smiled. And she smiled back.

He paid his check and went outside into the icy morning, then walked the familiar path to the trading post thinking about the pretty girl, Selene, and wondering if his friendless, empty existence in Gallup would change. Inside the store, he repeated the chores of opening the business, and as he walked toward the vault caught his reflection in a mirror on the jewelry counter.

Looking at himself, he smoothed his dark hair, and his brown eyes distanced as he thought of Selene again. Did she think he was good looking? He had been told that his Navajo and Caucasian bloods mixed well—though other Navajos teased him about looking like a *belagaana*—a White man. He always felt like a Navajo and never considered his other blood—until now.

***

Ben Monroe slipped out of bed just after dawn—even though he had come home late the night before—careful not to wake his wife. He felt guilty as he looked down at Cecelia. She was devoted to their daughter, though somewhat distant to him. He had time to fix that—later—he thought. Now it was time to make more money.

He went into the bathroom to shower and shave, and his thoughts drifted to last night remembering Karen and her sweet young body. He dressed quickly and admired himself in the mirror—strong and muscular at 39. He ran a comb through his dark hair. The hint of silver at the temples accented his chiseled features, and he was sure the girls liked him for more than his money. His rendezvous with Karen had become more complicated when he put Zia up in the apartment. But, since he had rented her a larger furnished apartment, Karen's favors were back on track.

Carrying his snakeskin cowboy boots, he stepped quietly down the hall toward the stairs and noticed Selene's door ajar. She would probably be in the kitchen with Luz—glad to be home for semester break.

At the foot of the stairs, the glow of sunrise filtered through the living room windows and angled across the dark stone floor spread with Navajo rugs—rugs from Ganado and Two Grey Hills. Massive leather couches sat in front of a huge stone fireplace where the mantle held several large pieces of Pueblo pottery—a black stone-polished platter by Maria Martinez from San Ildefonso, a carved and stone-polished red clay Santa Clara wedding vase by Teresita Naranjo and a large vase of muted natural clay paints by Feather Woman from Hopi. Ben loved this room. He had personally chosen the best rugs and pottery to showcase his home.

Ben tip-toed into the large, newly-remodeled kitchen—where Luz Luna, their live-in housekeeper of many years—who was like family—stood rolling tortillas with her back to him. When she heard the chair scrape the floor as Ben sat to put on his boots, she jumped and shrieked, "¡*Ay Dios mío!*"

Ben chuckled. Luz was afraid of everything—especially the *brujas*, the witches of New Mexico. She knew every witch story and lived in constant fear of an encounter. The family accepted her superstitions and switched between pacifying her to teasing her about the brujas.

Dressed in one of her many cotton housedresses, a crisp colorful apron, a bulky sweater and wearing sturdy shoes, Luz poured coffee for Ben as he reached across the rugged wooden table for the *Albuquerque Journal,* lighting his first Marlboro of the day.

"Luz, who won the Lobo-Aggie basketball game last night?"

"*No sé,*" she shrugged. "I hope it was the Aggies, because Lobos are just like coyotes—witches in disguise."

Ben just shook his head and thumbed through the paper for the sports section.

"Where's Selene? I thought she would be down here with you."

"She went to Boyd's. That girl was gnawing at the bit to eat green chile."

Ben shrugged, knowing she always misconstrued ordinary expressions.

"Anyway, I told her to be careful. It wasn't quite light out when she left, and she insisted on walking. I reminded her that's when Petra walks the streets carrying that little sack of *chicharones*, and to never take one if she offers."

Ben didn't comment, because he would have to hear about the long list of youngsters the bruja Petra had lured away with her sack of greasy pork rinds.

"*Por Dios Santo,*" she mumbled as she pulled the rosary from her apron pocket and blessed herself, kissed the cross then slipped it back into the pocket.

Luz poured Ben more coffee and served him a fresh warm tortilla that he slathered with butter and strawberry jam. He folded it in half and munched on it while sipping his coffee and scanning the newspaper.

"Remember, *Señor* Ben, this is the weekend I'm going to Albuquerque for my sister's 25th wedding anniversary. They're having a High Mass and they're going to recite their vowels again."

He didn't bother correcting her.

Ben finished his tortilla and slugged down the last of his coffee. He grabbed his leather jacket, darted out the kitchen door, jumped into the car and headed for Indian Jewelry Supply to buy silver chain for the pendants he had bought from the Arabs yesterday. He needed other findings and some cards for the sacks of earrings, too. Fortunately, they opened early. Every facet of the Indian jewelry business was booming, and the supply house was stocked full with the jewelry making and selling supplies that the silversmiths and retailers both needed.

He walked into the warehouse and headed for the counter to place his order. "I need 500 sterling silver chains—18-inch. Also, I'll take two gross of the sterling earring backs and a gross of earring wires. And I'll need a case of the black earring display cards…no, make it two cases."

While he waited for his order, he chatted with the owner about business and found out that one of his competitors had just bought a plane, because he was planning to do jewelry shows around the country.

"This is the best time we've ever seen in the Indian jewelry business. I sure hope it lasts," the owner said.

"Me, too," Ben agreed as his order arrived at the counter. He took the invoice off the package. "I'll have Louise drop a check off tomorrow morning on her way to the store."

Ben tossed the chain, findings and earring cards onto the back seat of the Lincoln and drove to the store puffing on a cigarette. He was pleased with how quickly Zia was learning the business and felt a sense of relief in the level of trust he had for his son. He desperately wanted to be a "real" father to him but didn't know how. Ben thought if he could mold Zia to become just like himself, then that would suffice for fatherhood.

He thought about how he had started into business when he was just 20, moving to Gallup and renting a small storefront on Route 66. His dad donated some inventory and he filled the store with inexpensive curios and touristy souvenirs like Indian headdresses, tomahawks and drums. He hired a Navajo artist to paint the front of the store with colorful thunderbirds, kachinas and rainbow *yei* dancers and letter "Indian Village" across the top of the building. Later he moved to the new location after he bought the building. He smiled at how far he had come.

His mind went back to current business—and his gut continued to tell him something wasn't quite right. Merchandise was turning so quickly, he couldn't put a finger on it—but he knew something was wrong. Someone was stealing. He was sure of it. He had to sharpen his instincts and pay better attention.

In the meantime, he wanted more accounts. He was working with a national jewelry chain that was interested in selling Indian jewelry in their stores, and he thought about maybe hiring someone to travel and sell to the gift shops and retailers around the southwest. He had the inventory. He just needed the right salesman.

***

Selene Monroe thought about her next semester at UNM as she strolled home after breakfast. Maybe she didn't want to be a teacher—get an education degree. She wanted something more exciting. But, what? At 19, she was in a big hurry to achieve her goals—whatever they might be. Her dad wanted her to learn the business, but she wasn't interested.

She was tired of his speech about how everyone in college became ants—followers, and how he could teach her to make money. Sure he had struck it rich as an Indian arts and crafts dealer. But that was his dream—not hers. Even though she benefitted from it, she had to follow her own dreams, although they were clouded at the moment. She just didn't want to become someone predictable. She wanted to be unique—out of the ordinary.

Luz jumped when Selene slipped in through the kitchen door, took off her jacket and rubbed her hands together for warmth.

"*Ay, qué frio,*" Selene said.

"You're going to catch your death of ammonia out there."

"It *is* freezing this morning. Anything happening around here, Luz?"

"No, *mijita*, it's deader than a doorknob. Your father left a little while ago, and I haven't seen your mother yet."

"Okay, then you can sit and have coffee with me, Luz, and give me some advice."

Luz poured two large mugs of brew and they sat together at the big wooden table like they had many times before. Luz had been Selene's advisor since she was a small child.

"I don't really know if I want to be a teacher anymore."

"Ay, Dios. You can do something else. Mijita, I've been with you since you were a baby, and I have a photogenic memory, and as far as I can remember, you didn't come with directions."

Selene sipped her coffee, and smiled, thinking about what Luz had said.

"Relax. You don't have to be in such a big hurry—abide your time. The only one who ever knew what they wanted to be was your father. According to him, he started working when he was a baby. He probably had a pocket in his diaper to hold the money."

"Oh, Luz," Selene giggled. "You're making me feel a little better already. I guess I'll figure out what I want. Maybe I should talk to my counselor and think about studying something else. Maybe I'm just getting nervous because what if I step out into the real world and don't like what I'm doing?"

"Mijita, remember, your mother named you 'Selene' after the moon goddess. So you have the force of the moon to guide you and give you strength, but you have to remember that the moon is always changing—so that means you are changeable…like the moon. Maybe that's why you're having such a hard time deciding what you want to be."

"Your mother named you '*Luz*' for the moon, too. Does that mean we have a spiritual connection?"

"Por Dios Santo, that's taken for granite."

Cecelia walked in, dressed in a smart black wool pant suit and black leather flats. Her long dark hair was pulled back and clipped at the base of her neck with a large hand-stamped Navajo sterling silver barrette. A fourth-generation New Mexican, Cecelia's soft features and gray eyes were typical of many of the Aragon family.

Selene, who resembled her exactly, thought she had a sophisticated look—never too much jewelry or too much makeup, but stylish and tailored.

"Mom, where are you headed so early all dressed up?"

"I volunteered for the committee to raise money for Gallup Catholic High. The school needs scholarships, and I said I would help out. Now they made me the head of fundraising, and I'm not sure what to do. That was after I told them to come up with something more creative than bake sales and car washes. So, now Mrs. Smarty Pants here has been designated chairman," she sighed. "I have time for a cup of coffee with the two of you. Have any fundraising ideas?"

Luz poured Cecilia a mug of coffee and refilled hers and Selene's. With a perplexed look she said, "Well CeCe, it looks like you just went from the fire into the frying pan. I can't think of a thing."

"Mom, I remember when I went there, they raffled a pickup. What about that—or a car? Or how about whoever donates the most money gets to put their name on a building. Dad and all the Indian traders would compete to give the most money."

"Well, Selene, you're right about the ego fest for the traders, but I'm not sure that's what the school wants. But keep thinking of ideas. For now, I have to go and face my committee and hope that one of them has an idea."

Cecilia slipped on her long wool coat, said her goodbyes and walked out the kitchen door and slid into the new red Mustang that Ben had just bought her and drove over to Gallup Catholic High School, the school she had attended when her family first moved to Gallup from Albuquerque. After graduating, she went to UNM in

Albuquerque and lived with her grandmother, affectionately called "the *abuelita*."

When Cecelia came home that first summer, she met Ben Monroe while she was waiting tables at the El Rancho Hotel. It was the local gathering place. The rustic hotel was built in the late '30s and billed as the world's largest ranch house and home to the famous movie stars who filmed the John Ford westerns in the area. Cecelia often came in early to wander around the rugged two-story lobby or go up the winding polished stairway with its log-pole railings to the mezzanine hoping to catch a glimpse of Spencer Tracy, Katharine Hepburn, Kirk Douglas or Henry Fonda, but that summer they weren't filming, so she would look at the signed, framed photographs that hung along the mezzanine wall showing "The Bad Man," starring Wallace Beery and Ronald Reagan or "Big Carnival," with Kirk Douglas and many more.

The only person she saw with star-like qualities was Ben Monroe. The first day he strolled into the restaurant, he caught her eye. Then, he said something to the cashier and pointed in Cecelia's direction and was quickly seated in her section. He stared at her as she fumbled for a menu and walked to his table. When she set the menu down, he slipped his hand over hers and whispered, "Our eyes met like magnets. Did you feel it, too?"

After that, Ben Monroe dined at the El Rancho every evening that Cecelia worked. He told her about his souvenir store on Route 66 and his future expectations.

"I'm going to be rich. I won't accept less from myself."

"Well, I'm just a college girl studying to be a social worker."

"College just *costs* money. It can't *make* you money."

"I've never heard that before, Ben."

"I suppose you're one of those fancy sorority girls?"

"No. I live with my grandmother in an old adobe house close to the campus. I work to help with tuition, but my parents help me, too."

Ben fascinated her with his unique approach to life and his zeal to make money. She was used to the more studious type of guy, like the graduate student she was dating in Albuquerque—she didn't mention him to Ben. She juggled both relationships for the next year. Then, on what seemed a whim to others, she drove off to Las Vegas with Ben Monroe where they got married. She quit college. Selene was born several months later.

She always cringed when people talked about secrets. Only Luz knew Cecelia's secret. Neither woman knew Ben's secret.

***

Anjelah Yazzie loved her reservation home. She lived close to her family—her clan. The only time she had ever been away was when she was forced to attend Navajo boarding school. She learned a lot there, but the loneliness was unbearable. She missed her family and longed for her traditional life—the life that the boarding school was trying to change.

Like many Navajos, the Yazzies raised sheep, and, as a youngster, her mother had taught Anjelah to weave. She helped haul water and chop wood, and her father showed her how to butcher sheep.

Her father was a silversmith, and his outdoor shop consisted of a tree stump, a hammer, a chisel and a blow torch. "This is all I need," he told her. From his simple workshop, he fashioned silver into rings and bracelets and set polished turquoise stones in the hand-formed bezels.

Her mother's rug weaving post was also located outside their family hogan. The vertical loom made of tree branches stood against a juniper tree. A large basket stuffed with bundles of natural yarn and tools sat nearby. It held everything from sheep shears and wire-toothed wool carders, to a long spindle which her mother used to deftly spin the yarn, and hand-whittled hardwood combs whose tines matched the spacing of the warp threads on her loom. A cast iron pot was used to boil various herbs that she used to create the natural dyes and earthy colors for her hand-spun yarn.

"From sheep to rug," Anjelah would say as she watched and learned to weave the banded rugs that her mother and grandmother wove. One of the earliest weaving styles, they were known for the horizontal bands of multi-colored diamond designs or chevrons, the v-shaped patterns. Anjelah blamed the years at boarding school for never fully developing her skill as a rug weaver.

The summer after her junior year at boarding school, she got a job at Red Cliffs Trading Post in Thoreau. The owner liked to have Navajos working in the store, because that's what the tourists wanted to see. Anjelah found the sightseers rather strange—like they expected to see the movie version of an Indian chief ride in on horseback adorned in buckskins and a headdress, raising his hand to say "How."

She worked side-by-side with the owner's son, Ben Monroe, pricing souvenirs and curios, stocking shelves, learning to use the cash register and make proper change. Ben was energetic and fun to be around—and she liked the way his dark hair formed soft waves, and his warm brown eyes lit up every time a grin spread across his face—yes, he was strong and good looking for a White guy. At least he wasn't pale and pasty like some of those teenagers vacationing with their parents—especially those spotted ones—staring at Indians for the first time. She told Ben they looked odd, but he laughed and told her those spots were called freckles, and a lot of White people had them.

Sometimes after they closed the store, Ben would drive Anjelah home, and when they became better friends, they headed out the winding dirt road toward Bluewater Lake for a picnic or drove farther into the Zuni Mountains to Ojo Redondo where the summer rain had transformed it into a lush green meadow. If they were quiet, they could see mule deer, elk or turkey. And in August they picked wild raspberries.

Ben shared his lofty plans and expectations. Anjelah had never known anyone like Ben and quickly became infatuated with him—her first love.

When she discovered she was pregnant, the shame overwhelmed her.

Her parents were shocked but quickly became supportive, and her clan accepted her child as one of them. They helped build a small hogan close by her parents' dwelling, where she could care for her child.

Ben's folks insisted he take financial responsibility and, in the meantime, they helped provide enough money for her to get by, and later Ben's dad gave Anjelah his old International pickup when he bought a new truck. They rarely saw their grandson or got to know him, and Anjelah never worked in the store again. Soon, Ben opened his first store in Gallup and took over financial responsibility.

Anjelah was determined her child would not be an outcast.

***

Zia made arrangements to see his counselor and began plans to move from his Albuquerque apartment. When he told Ben he was taking the bus to Albuquerque on his day off, Ben offered Zia the use of the store's truck.

"While you're there I want you to go to Strings O' Silver and pick up my order of liquid silver. And I'll call Palms Trading and request a nice selection of pottery—make the trip worthwhile. Besides, you'll get to meet some of the people we do business with."

The following morning, Zia drove east out of Gallup as the pink dawn burst into a tangerine sky and bathed the vast landscape in sunshine. He recited the Beauty Way prayer from the driver's seat of the truck instead of from the front door of the hogan:

> *With beauty before me I walk.*
> *With beauty behind me I walk.*
> *With beauty below me I walk.*

With beauty above me I walk.
With beauty all around me I walk.
I will be happy forever.

He faltered when he said "I will be happy forever." He didn't feel sincere saying it now.

By the time Zia met with his counselor, she had already researched his situation.

"Zia, I've talked to the dean and your department chair, and I think we've come up with a solution for you. We don't want to lose you so close to graduation. You've always been an excellent student, and we see a lot of promise in you."

"So, Dr. Ortiz, what do I need to do?"

"We've decided to create an area of independent study that will fill the final requirements for your education theory classes. Now, it won't be easy. It's almost like a thesis—a fast-paced thesis," Ramona Ortiz said.

Zia squirmed, feeling nervous.

"Okay, can you explain it a little more?"

"You will present a written proposal to our committee with an outline of your independent study project, and we will approve it if it satisfies the necessary criteria for your degree in education."

Zia's idea was percolating, but it would take some development.

"You will be required to meet with us every two weeks to submit your written progress and for our critique, discussion and suggestions."

Zia hoped Ben would need a lot of merchandise from

Albuquerque.

"I really appreciate what you're doing for me. I know this is a big undertaking, and I promise I won't disappoint you."

He looked away, out the window. He knew he couldn't ask Ben for tuition money. How was he going to pull this off?

"What's wrong, Zia, are you having second thoughts?"

"Oh...no...no, Dr. Ortiz." He stood silently for a minute. "It's the tuition I'm worried about. My situation has changed, and I don't have tuition paid for me any longer."

"Zia, you forget, I'm a counselor. I help people with grants, loans and scholarships. Let me get to work for you."

"You would do that for me?"

"Of course. Now get your ideas in order. Classes start two weeks from today, and we need your proposal here in my office by next week. Hopefully, by then I'll have some funding lined up for you."

She gave him the rest of the details and requirements, and Zia set the appointment time for the following week and left feeling exhilarated...but nervous. This was the opportunity he needed to get his degree. He wanted to use this independent study to create an educational concept for the Navajo reservation. That had always been his dream. Now he had to put his idea on paper—make it real.

He hopped into the truck and headed for his rounds picking up merchandise. First he stopped for the liquid silver. It made sense that the smooth look and feel of it gave it the name "liquid silver." He knew how well it was selling, but it wasn't really handmade Indian jewelry—though it was hand-strung in multi-strands, waterfalls and graduated strands. Sure it was stylish with the silver tubing interspersed with turquoise and coral heishi beads, but it wasn't traditional. I guess I'm a purist, Zia thought, as he looked at the ring his grandfather had made him.

Driving toward Old Town, he stopped at Palms Trading Company, where an order of Pueblo pottery was packed and waiting for him. He met the owner and crew and wandered through the store—noticing everything in a more educated way.

After they loaded up the carefully wrapped pottery, he drove a few blocks to Duran's Pharmacy. Their café section at the far end of the drug store was a local favorite. Zia ordered a bowl of spicy, meaty green chile with pinto beans and a homemade flour tortilla—hot off the grill—slathered with butter. He enjoyed every mouthful.

Since none of his friends or roommates was in town yet, he decided to head back to Gallup and stop to see his mother along the way and give her the good news. Now that he would be coming back to Albuquerque every few weeks, he decided to keep up his share of the rent—then he'd have a place to stay and keep his things in order. Besides, Ben didn't even charge him rent for the Gallup apartment. He was very generous.

Zia started Ben's truck and headed west on I-40 for the trip home. He wondered what tourists thought when they experienced the openness that lay ahead. For him, the rugged landscape and giant sky were part of his soul, his family history. He was glad his mother had named him Zia. Though the Pueblo name was symbolic of the sun, the sun symbol also stood for a clear mind, strong body, pure spirit and devotion to the welfare of the tribe. He hoped he could live up to his name.

About an hour-and-a-half later, he rolled off the Thoreau exit and glanced over toward Ben's parents' store. He never really knew them, so they didn't feel like grandparents. How odd.

He stopped at the small local market and bought a few groceries that his mother would probably need and drove out toward the red rock hillside. He never tired of the terra cotta cliffs or the clear blue sky—especially when it was tossed with clouds. The sandstone folds of the mountains were sheer and dramatic.

He took the dirt road up to his mother's hogan. He passed the place where the Begay family's sheep always grazed—the Navajo churro sheep were a sound and hearty breed. The old grandmother was herding the sheep toward home, sounding her makeshift rattle— a tin can filled with pebbles, held by a string—encouraging the sheep to move. He thought about his own grandmother whose age was determined by the fact that she was born when the corn was about as high as his childhood knee—so that would probably have been May or June, and they figured she was around 70. Zia was proud and amazed that she still herded sheep and rode a horse.

When he was a small boy, his grandparents would take him in their horse-drawn wagon on trips for supplies—Blue Bird flour, beans, lard and canned goods. The movement of the horses rocked the wagon along the rutted red-dirt path to town. As they bumped along he would gaze at the junipers and piñons—trees twisted by years of constant wind and weather. They stood as hearty as his

Navajo people who were the soul of the environment.

He especially loved to go with them in the fall—in a year when the pines produced a crop of nuts and the landscape was blanketed with yellow and purple brush. You would see Navajo wagons near the stands of trees.

First they would place blankets around the base of a tree—then shake it so the ripe cones would fall onto the blankets. Then the hard work began. Nestled inside each segment of the cone was a small dark pine nut. And each segment had to be opened by hand to encourage the piñon out of hiding. It was a labor-intensive and pine-sap-sticky chore. But it was a cash crop that his grandfather sold to a local store.

Of course, his grandfather always gave him a bundle to take home to his mother. She would roast the tiny nuts in a cast iron skillet on the wood stove, first putting a little water and salt in the pan to toast a layer of nuts. As they cooled, Zia would grab a handful and break into each nut with a quick snap of his teeth. Roasting brought out the wonderful flavor of the cream-colored nuggets.

Daydreaming his way home, Zia pulled up in front of the hogan and parked next to his mother's old faded blue pickup. Anjelah looked surprised to see him jump out of Ben's truck.

They talked over coffee and munched on soda crackers and Vienna sausages from the small can he had bought at the market. He told her about the special arrangement his counselor had made for him to finish his final semester.

"It's almost like a thesis. I have to create a proposal, do the research and present my findings and results to the department every few weeks while I'm in the process. It won't be easy, but you know how I've always felt about education on the reservation. So that's my subject—improving the education system for the Navajo reservation."

"Well, Son, that seems like a big undertaking. What does your father say?"

"I haven't told him yet."

"Do you think he'll let you go to Albuquerque every two weeks?"

"I have days off. I won't let it interfere with my job at the store. I work weekends, so my days off are during the week. My counselor is working on a grant or scholarship for me, too, so I don't have to ask Ben for tuition money."

"It sounds wonderful, Son."

"I've been fortunate to go to college…and, well it's finally going to be time for me to stop my complaining about our people and our education and do something. I know it won't be easy and will take time—but I want to do it."

"Well, I hope it's not just a dream you put down on paper for your college teachers, Son. I really hope somehow it will come true."

That's what he had been worrying about as he drove from Albuquerque. What if he was just an idealistic student with lofty goals? What if he got caught up in the Gallup world-of-business and let his dreams slip away?

***

Back in Gallup, Zia delivered the merchandise to the store and helped unpack, mark and display the pottery and put the order of liquid silver necklaces in the vault to price later. He laughed when he picked up a heavy pot wrapped in disposable diapers. When he unwrapped the beautiful stone-polished black vase, he knew why. A large carved water serpent wound around the middle of the perfectly executed piece by Teresita Naranjo. She was a Santa Clara potter whose work was renowned and collected—and very expensive.

Soon, it was time to close the store, and Ben had asked Zia to leave the truck parked in front and put the keys on his desk. Zia walked toward Boyd's for dinner, thinking about his project at UNM and he felt a renewed spirit about his situation.

Gallup felt more familiar now, and he was developing an appreciation for the town. It seemed to have a live-and-let-live attitude. He liked the way the different cultures and ethnicities blended in the diverse landscape. It had its own unique charm—though he didn't think anyone would drive into Gallup and say, "Oh what a beautiful town."

He learned that when Route 66 first stretched through town in 1926, Gallup became a hub for travelers and the center of trade for the Indian artisans in the area. Long before that, it had been established as a coal mining and railroad town. In the 1880s when the railroad pushed west, a payroll office was established along a dusty length of tracks. The paymaster's name was David Gallup. So, when the railroaders headed to pick up their paychecks they would say, "I'm going to Gallup." And the name stuck.

Zia enjoyed that interesting fact, knowing that a lot of old western towns were named after railroaders. Even the town close to his reservation home, Thoreau, was named after a railroader. Many people thought it was after the poet/essayist—but you always knew who the locals were because they pronounced it "through."

After a burger and fries, he stepped into the chilly evening and walked to his apartment to start the outline for his project presentation. He would have to hire a typist. Maybe Louise knew someone.

***

"Bitchin', far out!" Karen Johnson sped east on I-40 toward Albuquerque in the new green Ford Mustang that Ben had bought for her at Gurley Motors. The radio was cranked up and she sang along with Mac Davis' hit song, "Oh, Lord, it's hard to be humble." That's me through and through, she thought.

It was her day off, and she planned to go straight to the mall, Winrock Shopping Center, and buy a few groovy new outfits at Dillard's and few more enticing things at Frederick's of Hollywood. She had to keep Ben Monroe interested. She wanted more than a car and pricey Indian jewelry for her romantic efforts. This was her opportunity to get ahead—whatever it took.

No more trailer parks for Karen. At 23, she had left her drunken boyfriend passed out in the trailer in Amarillo. She quietly put her clothes and a few other belongings in the back seat of her Corvair and headed to California with dreams of stardom. After all, she had good looks, a voluptuous figure, a great singing voice, and she knew she could act.

Her car made it as far as Gallup and broke down along Route 66, next to the railroad tracks and across the street from Monroe Trading Company. She jumped out and stared at the black smoke spewing from of the back of the car. "Why did I buy this damn Ralph Nader Special...shit car."

She kicked the driver's side door shut and stomped across the street—no phone booths in sight. But who would she call, anyway? Tears welled in her blue eyes as Karen stepped into an Indian arts and crafts store.

"You look like you're lost," the man behind the counter said.

"My car just broke down, and I don't know what to do. I'm moving to California. Is there a mechanic around here who could look at it?"

"Sure. I'll give my mechanic a call. What kind of a car is it?"

"A '65 Corvair."

"A '65 Corvair? Hmm...well, let's see if we can help a pretty girl today. I'm Ben Monroe." He offered her a hearty handshake and looked deeply into her eyes.

"I'm Karen Johnson."

He placed his left hand over their clasped hands. "Our eyes met like magnets. Did you feel it, too?"

***

When Jerry Davis slid into his car after work, he puffed on his

Marlboro. He'd usually stop for a cocktail at different bars—trying to find a place where people like him enjoyed a drink together.

I hate this hell-hole, dump of a town, he thought, as he drove east on Route 66 toward the trailer park. All I wanted to do was to get out of San Antonio and away from that love triangle that almost ruined my life—go someplace where nobody knew me. Maybe I should have kept going toward San Francisco. Now I'm stuck with a bunch of cowboys and Indians and worst of all those Arab sons-of-bitches. They're always kissing Ben's ass, "You're like my brother," or "I swear to God, I'm giving you this jewelry at my cost." What bullshit.

I need to make some money and move on, he thought. I know how to sell, that's why Ben hired me. But if he would pay me commission, I could stockpile some cash and move somewhere I fit in.

Instead of looking for a new bar, Jerry stopped at California Supermarket for a 6-pack of beer and a frozen pizza, then drove on to the trailer he had rented at the end of town. While the pizza baked, he had a couple of beers and waited for "Dallas" to come on television. He envied J.R. Ewing. He guessed he envied Ben Monroe, too…for all the things he had.

But what did *he* really want? What was he running away *from*? What was he running *to*? That affair had dealt him a blow that changed everything—ripped away the façade he had created.

***

Zia admitted that it was nice to get a paycheck, and Ben had signed for a pickup truck for him at Gurley Motors. Zia was responsible for the payments, and having a truck gave him a new sense of freedom—or maybe another form of entrapment. He was busy preparing his proposal for UNM, and on his day off, he drove the 45-minute trip to Thoreau to visit his mother, taking her food and supplies she couldn't get there. He planned to enjoy the peace and quiet of the reservation, and read and refine his hand-written proposal and gather his thoughts. He needed to complete it. Louise said she would type it for him during slow times between deposits, payroll and bookkeeping chores. Ben said that was okay. Zia had finally told him about the graduation project.

"You can do whatever you want with college as long as you don't miss work," he stated. "Give me your best while you're in this store. Our next project is updating our merchandising, and you're in charge."

On his visit with his mother, Zia caught himself talking about the business with some enthusiasm. He told her he was realizing there were lots of ways to learn things and Ben was teaching him well. He never mentioned anything to Anjelah about Ben and Karen, but he told her that he had yet to see any of Ben's "real" family. Zia remained cautious and never asked questions about Ben's wife or children. He didn't want to seem too curious, and nobody at the store mentioned anything either—not even Louise.

"The man is a workaholic—he probably hardly ever sees his *real* family." But, Zia had to admit, "Ben is quite generous.

Zia sat on the bench under a piñon tree outside the hogan to work on his project. It's the same place he did his homework growing up—the place where he would daydream about being a star basketball player for the Thoreau High School Hawks. His mother had made education a priority, so he did well in school—and he wore his basketball letter sweater proudly.

He jotted down notes and was deep in thought.

Reservation children are sent to school like they are going to a foreign country. They need a new program to jump start their learning and teach them the social skills they need in an educational environment.

Navajo kids are learning to be lazy.

Can we teach our children in the Navajo Way and still provide them a good schooling and have educated people?

I don't want to create another bureaucratic agency that functions for the agency itself and stands behind a long list of ideals but gets nowhere, he thought.

I watch the Navajos come into the store to sell their jewelry. They're clever and know how to negotiate. That's good instinct. I see their children tagging along. Some should be in school, but aren't. They are distant and unaware, though secure in their families and traditions. They need the sound values of Navajo language, tradition, family unity and clan identity, but they need to be able to step out of that world and learn other things and blend all of this to produce a new and better people. They're starting to lose some of their language and not learning English well either. They're quickly becoming illiterate in two languages.

What strength can a nation have if language and culture are diluted like old coffee re-percolated with used grounds producing a watery tasteless brew?

We are the Diné—the People.

You mustn't assume that all these children really understand the Navajo language and the Navajo Way. Maybe we need to be like the Catholic schools, teach the Navajo language and Navajo Way the same as Catholic kids learn Catechism.

Thoughts were shooting in all directions: If it's all blended together in a cohesive program, could he even pull this off? Was it just a bunch of rhetoric?

Knowledge is Power. The force of good overpowers the force of evil.

Sports are another great outlet—for energy, competition, success and interacting with other children.

It is important to take the children to favorite places—the places of their ancestors and their legends—the places that later they can revisit in their minds by simply closing their eyes.

The Navajo nation cannot increase its wealth by dividing its resources and continuing a lower standard of education.

Zia closed his notebook. He had a lot of work to do.

***

Louise Langley stayed in her office after the store closed to type Zia's proposal. Her IBM Selectric purred as her fingers glided over the keys. She liked the correction tape accessory, so she could easily correct a typo. She hoped it looked good to Zia, so she didn't have to retype the whole thing. Louise became enthralled with his ideas as she read and typed. He was such a nice young man and a hard worker. She was glad that he was getting an education and wouldn't be stuck working in an Indian arts and crafts store forever. She would.

Her husband, Fred, had diabetes and it was getting worse. Now he couldn't manage the cross-country truck driving anymore, so Louise volunteered to work more hours. Ben admitted he needed extra help. In addition to her bookkeeping duties, he paid her extra to check in the inventory against the invoices and help mark jewelry and keep the vault properly stocked for the wholesalers.

Louise worried constantly. The doctor told Fred that the circulation in his legs had worsened from the diabetes and he might need to have his left leg amputated below the knee. "I just don't understand this darn diabetes," Fred would say. "I thought if I cut down on the sugar and watched my diet that was it. Now they tell me they're gonna cut off my leg and maybe I'll go blind." He was discouraged.

She and Fred were still two years away from retirement, so she had to work harder. At least it was just the two of them. She had always been frugal, and they had some savings. But Fred needed to work at something part time so he wouldn't feel so useless.

***

When Zia unlocked the entrance to the store the next morning, Louise was already there.

A big smile spread across her face as she handed him the proposal for the Navajo Arts and Crafts Academy.

"Zia, I hope this looks okay. If not, I can make corrections and re-type the pages that need changes. By the way, your concept is brilliant. How did you come up with it?"

"Well, I've always wanted to improve education on the reservation…I had a completely different idea before I started working here. Suddenly, it made sense to combine the two concepts. Well, you read it; I don't need to over-explain."

"I just have one question, Zia. Why are you working here anyway?"

Zia shoved his hands into the pockets of his Wranglers.

"Well, Louise, that's a long story that I just can't go into right now."

"Since the first day you came to work, there's been something familiar about you, but I could never put my finger on it."

"You're just around too many Navajos, Louise."

She cracked a smile. "I guess so."

Zia insisted on paying Louise for her typing, and he couldn't wait to study his proposal carefully. He only had two days left until his meeting at UNM. He knew he couldn't scrutinize it until after work, so he put it in a manila envelope and set in on the counter in the vault and got to work on his new merchandising project.

Lately, he was beginning to feel like the store manager. Ben gave him more responsibility. He planned to visit a few fine jewelry stores in Albuquerque on Thursday after his meeting. Maybe he could get some merchandising and display ideas.

Ben had left for Albuquerque earlier and would fly to Dallas for a few days—hopefully making his deal to sell Indian jewelry to a fine jewelry chain.

Jerry and Karen were straightening up the store before it got busy, bickering at each other as usual.

"Don't get your undies in a bunch, Karen. So what if Ben hasn't paid enough attention to you lately. He's a workaholic, and you're acting like a damn whore. See for yourself…here." Jerry grabbed a mirror off the counter stepped back and made a sweeping motion toward Karen. "He's given you so much Indian jewelry you're starting to look like a Christmas tree."

"You asshole," she screeched.

Karen stomped across the wood plank floor to a set of showcases full of trays of rings and began rearranging them the way Ben had suggested—all the Zuni inlay, cluster and needlepoint together, all the Navajo single and double stone turquoise and coral rings together, and the Hopi silver overlay in trays of their own. Ben had no patience for rings. He said customers took forever trying them on, getting the right size. "You can sell five pairs of earrings or a stack of pendants faster than one ring," he would say.

Sometimes it feels like babysitting with these two, Zia thought. Jerry has a chip on his shoulder and he takes it out on Karen—and he gets to her every time.

Then, two buyers Zia recognized as owners of Arizona Wholesale Indian Jewelry in Phoenix strolled in with a purpose. Frank and Bob were excellent customers, and he would give them all the attention they needed. With Zia's assistance, a few hours later they had an excellent selection. While they were at lunch, Zia sorted everything according to retail price then wrote up the itemized invoice, totaled it and deducted their jobbers' discount. When they returned, he went over the invoice with them, and they wrote the check and took their packages.

But something was bothering Zia.

"Hey Jerry, Karen, didn't we have a whole bag of those Effie Calavaza bracelets?"

"Who's Effie Calavaza?" Karen asked, looking clueless.

"Jeez, how long have you worked here? Jerry said. "She's the one from Zuni who sets the turquoise and coral nuggets in thick silver bezels and always has a silver snake running through the design."

"Nope," Karen shook her head. "Don't know anything about it."

"Me neither," answered Jerry.

Is this what Ben was worried about? Zia was certain that the bag of bracelets was there yesterday—and they were expensive. He had to watch more carefully. At least now he knew enough to pay better attention.

Soon it was closing time, and he checked out the register, put the bank bag in the vault and grabbed his proposal. He locked the vault door with a quick spin of the combination, and followed the crew out the front door, setting the alarm before he closed and locked the store.

Zia couldn't wait to examine the proposal. He walked to Boyd's with a purpose. There he could get a quick dinner and sit while going over it thoroughly. When he stepped inside, he saw a group of Arabs at the back table under their usual cloud of smoke—the table scattered with empty plates and coffee mugs. They waved in recognition, and he knew he had to greet them.

"Hello, my good man. How's business?"

Zia shook hands and made some small talk about business. These people were natural merchants. They lived to do business. No wonder Ben liked them so much.

He excused himself and sat at a booth close to the front of the restaurant where he could concentrate. A bowl of posole—hominy stew with pork and red chile—sounded appetizing.

He stared at the title page: Navajo Arts and Crafts Academy. Was his idea too brazen—outrageous?

What would the committee think? Well, it's too late now. I have to give it a try, he thought.

While he waited for the posole, he studied the package. Louise had done a great job of typing and organizing the material in outline form. It looked professional.

What a nice woman, that Louise. She wasn't annoying like Jerry and Karen.

His posole arrived with a thick warm tortilla, and he put his papers aside while he enjoyed the hearty regional specialty. While he ate, he realized that lately he was learning more than he expected—doors of knowledge flung open in places he never would have gone before.

Just then the café door opened and the pretty girl he had seen there before appeared with a woman who had to be her mother and a chubby lady bundled up in an old-fashioned coat wearing sturdy shoes. The mother was dressed in a wool sweater, slacks and loafers. Zia tried not to stare at the girl who wore a denim shirt and jeans with a small link concho belt wound through the loops of the jeans, black leather boots and a soft black leather jacket. She looked even prettier than the last time he saw her.

"Well, look who's here, Cecelia, Selene and Luz," the waitress said. "Did you come in for dinner?"

"Yes, my husband is out of town on business, and we decided on a girls' night out at Boyd's."

"Well then, sit down here, and I'll get you something to drink while you decide on your dinners," she said, placing menus in front of them.

"We're all about coffee," Selene said.

"Good timing, I just made a fresh pot."

Zia sat directly across from them, and gulped down a spoonful of posole while he stared at Selene. Would she look at him? Would she remember him?

When their coffee arrived, the ladies were ready to order.

"I'll have a bowl of green chile with beans," said Cecelia.

"Me, too" added Selene. "My favorite."

"Well, I'm no 'copier cat,' so I'll have the stacked blue corn enchiladas with red chile and a fried egg on top," chimed Luz.

Just then, the Arabs—on their way out of the restaurant—stopped at the table. Their leader bowed and said, "Hello, missus. Hello, Selene, and you, lovely lady," he said to Luz. "Good to see you all."

After his gracious hellos, the Arab leader headed to the counter, paid his check and handed the waitress what looked like a $20 tip and left.

"Are those Arabs? Are they from the 'Syanide Peninsula' or something?" Luz asked.

Selene nearly choked on her coffee.

"No, Luz. Dad said they are Palestinians from the West Bank and maybe some from Gaza."

"Hmm," Luz shrugged.

"So, Mom, what's happening with your committee at school? Did you come up with any good ideas for fund raising?"

"Not really. So far the only plan is we're going to sell World's Finest Chocolate and then have a booth at Ceremonials this summer and do a silent auction. We'll get some of the traders to donate jewelry—nice things, like squash blossoms and concho belts."

"Gee, just what everybody needs around here, more Indian jewelry. And World's Finest Chocolate—I thought you wanted something original."

Selene snapped her fingers. "Darn," she shook her head. "It's too bad you didn't start your campaign sooner, you could have sold tamales for Christmas and made a fortune."

"What a great idea, Selene. Maybe we can do that next year."

Their food arrived, and as the waitress was setting the orders in front of them, Selene took a quick look across to the next booth and caught Zia's glance and smiled. He smiled back.

Maybe she recognized me, he thought. He pushed the empty bowl aside and pulled the proposal out to study and consider every angle.

Soon, he was lost in his concept and found a few things that needed to be changed. It would mean Louise would have to re-type a couple of pages. As he crossed out and edited, from beside the booth he heard, "Homework?"

Zia looked up and at Selene. Cecelia and Luz were scooting out of the booth.

"Well…ah, yes. I have to get this ready before classes start next week."

"Oh, so you're at UNM?"

Zia nodded.

"Me, too. I'm majoring in education for now…I guess."

"So am I. If this goes well," he said holding up the proposal, "I'll graduate in May."

"Maybe I'll see you around campus. My name is Selene," she said, extending her hand.

"I'm Zia Yazzie, he said offering her a hearty handshake. Even though it wasn't a Navajo custom, shaking hands had become natural for him.

"See you later. They're waiting for me."

Selene hurried to the door to catch up with her mother and Luz.

"Who was that cute guy, Selene?"

"Oh, I've seen him here before, Mom, alone…uh, and just thought I'd talk to him."

"There's something familiar about him," Luz grimaced, buttoning her coat. Do you believe in reincarnation?"

"Oh please, Luz. Hey, maybe he's the son of that bruja, Petra, and was raised on chicharones," Selene quipped.

"Enough, ladies. The car is across the street in front of the theater. We have to stop at the market on our way home. Luz, you have the list, right?"

"Of course."

"Luz, before I go back to school will you make sopaipillas? Yours are the best...yum, hot fried dough filled with as much honey as possible."

"Sure. And you'll call your friends to come over and they'll be gone in five minutes. All that work. Ay Dios."

PART 2: LAND OF ENCHANTMENT

Ben Monroe snapped the seat belt for his flight to Dallas. A jewelry case in the overhead compartment held trays stacked with an assortment of Indian jewelry to show the buyer for O'Malley's Gems & Jewels, a discount fine jewelry chain.

It was nearly dusk as the plane lifted off, and he gazed down at the expanding city of Albuquerque, stretching north and east, then out toward Sandia Peak towering above the town. He settled in, ordered a Scotch and soda, and started flirting with the stewardess.

Boy, I've come a long way from that kid growing up in Thoreau, he thought.

He reminisced about how in 1931 his parents left the Dust Bowl of Oklahoma and drove west along the unpaved stretch of Route 66 until their jalopy broke down in Thoreau, New Mexico—all their belongings were stuffed inside the old Hudson and a lumpy feather mattress covered in striped ticking was tied to the roof. They had a small dowry and nothing else. His father was an instinctively smart man—a self-proclaimed preacher of farmer stock from Oklahoma, and his mother, a farm girl herself, was always at his side.

Fortunately for them, Thoreau sat in what was called the "checkerboard area," an expanse where deeded land and reservation land were interspersed—and that offered them potential business possibilities. They were able to make a small down payment on an old stone building that sat along Route 66.

At first, his father thought he could set up a missionary church and convert the Navajos.

What Matthew and Melba Monroe soon discovered was that the Navajos needed groceries and dry goods more than Christianity. They converted the old stone building that housed their makeshift church and small living quarters into a store that sold canned goods— stewed tomatoes, peaches, condensed milk—flour, sugar, lard, beans and coffee. They continued to live in the small quarters behind the store where they struggled and prayed, putting every penny back into merchandise. The store faced a dusty stretch of Route 66. The railroad tracks ran east and west just north of where the store sat, and the vast Zuni Mountains appeared limitless to the south.

Little by little they learned more about what the Navajos wanted and needed and adapted their merchandise, including bolts of velvet in deep red, cobalt and burgundy, even denim jeans. Then they added lanterns and oil, tin-ware bowls and mugs.

Ben remembered his mother telling him about her garden. After enduring their first freezing winter in the searing wind and non-stop blizzards, she decided she needed to plant a garden. But, where would she get the seed? There was enough corn and beans in the area.

"My papa told me the old settlers in Oklahoma would just shoot down a few of those migrating geese from Canada and cut the grain from their gullets to plant, so that's what your daddy and me did," she told Ben as he sat on her knee as a youngster. "I had the best garden in all of the Zuni Mountains."

She would chuckle that when the Navajos saw her rows of oats, wheat and barley, they looked like they almost believed there was something magical in that Bible of Matthew's after all.

Ben was born in 1935, and by then Route 66 had more travelers.

"Them cars looked like giant black beetles crawling along the road," Matthew would say.

Sometimes the cars stopped at the store. The tourists would get out look around like they were expecting to see something unique— then leave. That's when Matthew got the idea to start carrying curios and souvenirs. He even traded for some turquoise and silver jewelry the Navajos created. When word got around that he was buying jewelry, Navajos would come to the store with their wares wrapped in a calico cloth and sit on the benches outside until they felt the time was right to approach Matthew. To the Navajos, it was rude to simply walk into the store and aggressively try to sell something. His dad learned their habits, and he learned to speak some trader Navajo as well.

The more Matthew developed his skill at merchandising and selling, the more business the store did. Soon curios, souvenirs and Indian jewelry and crafts totally replaced the groceries and dry goods. By then another market had filled those needs. He finally put a name on the storefront, "Red Cliffs Trading Post," and had a local artist paint wooden cut-outs of rainbow dancers and thunderbirds and anchored them against the stone structure to attract tourists. He added gas pumps. That really helped business. Matthew was always checking the glass receptacles at the top of the gravity-fed pumps pumped them back up to ten gallons whenever necessary.

Ben worked in the store from the time he could stand on a wooden crate and see over the knotty pine counter. He learned to add like a whiz and could make correct change before he lost his first tooth.

"I love money, Daddy," he stated one day.

"Now, Son, the Bible says it ain't proper to love money."

"Well, it sure seems proper to me."

Ben was glad he had that simple upbringing. His mother taught him to read and write even before he went to the small local school.

He learned math working in the store, and he learned to speak some Navajo and to respect and understand the culture from his classmates and the people of his surroundings. That's probably why he didn't take to his folks' Bible religion. And he was determined not to talk like an Okie. He listened to the way the tourists spoke, and he paid attention to the voices on the radio when his dad tuned in the news and the boxing matches—or listened to serials.

He enjoyed listening to the Navajos, too. They had funny ways of saying things. His dad had installed a crank-up phone in the store that connected directly to the operator. One morning a Navajo woman came to use the phone and after his dad cranked it for her she said with her guttural Navajo accent, "Hello, operations, give me long way."

Of course Ben knew he had picked up expressions, too. The Navajos copied colloquial expressions like "Long time no see." That probably didn't make any sense to them and it became "Long time no look."

His dad liked having Navajos around for the tourists to see, and he always hired them to work in the store—especially in the summer. Sammy Largo would walk to work from miles out on the reservation. Every morning when he arrived, he'd come through the door, stop and take a deep breath and say, "It's tiredness already."

That summer when the beautiful Anjelah Yazzie worked in the store, it was a shock to his parents when Ben got her pregnant. They were embarrassed and ashamed. But nobody could change the outcome.

Yes, you've come a long way, he thought as the pilot announced their approach to Dallas.

***

Zia sat outside his counselor's office. He was glad the proposal was tucked into a large manila envelope. With his hands sweating the way they were, he would have wrinkled the crisp white watermarked paper that Louise had chosen to type it on. "Quality paper makes a good impression," she insisted.

What will they think? What will they ask? He was worried about the meeting. He was worried about the store. With Ben in Dallas, he hoped Louise could watch over Karen and Jerry. He didn't trust either one of them.

As the door opened, he could hear Dr. Ortiz speaking with her usual enthusiasm. "Now if you're still not convinced that teaching is for you after this semester, then change majors before you have too many credits in education."

Zia stood, waiting his turn.

Ramona Ortiz walked out of her office and the girl following said, "Thank you, Dr. Ortiz. I guess I just want something more exciting out of life."

Suddenly, he was face to face with Selene.

"Hi," she said, surprised.

"You know Zia, Selene?" Dr. Ortiz said.

"Yes, we met in Gallup."

"Well, I'll tell you, if you have any questions or doubts about getting your degree in education, you should talk to him. He could give you some insight."

An embarrassed grin crept across Zia's face.

"Good idea, Dr. Ortiz," she said as she winked at Zia.

He gulped. "Sure, any time, Selene."

"How about today?"

"Well, I have a meeting with Dr. Ortiz, and I don't know how long it will take."

"Our meeting will be over in about an hour, so you two could meet any time after 11:00," she announced, looking from her watch to Zia and picking up his obvious attraction to Selene,

Suddenly he felt trapped into a commitment by these two women.

"Okay, how about 11:30 across from campus at the Frontier?" he choked out the words in fear of rejection.

"Perfect," agreed Selene.

"Green chile?" he said with a smile.

"Always. See you there."

Now I'm really nervous, he thought. Two challenges instead of just one.

The dean and department chair approached chatting about class registration figures and which courses they would have to cancel or combine because of low enrollment before the semester started.

"Whenever things are thriving, our enrollment goes down. We do better during recessions."

Zia nervously tucked the freshly laundered cowboy shirt into the new Wranglers. His cowboy boots were polished. Ben was a stickler for polished shoes.

He took a deep breath and walked into the conference room.

The two men and Ramona Ortiz were already studying his proposal and jotted notes on legal pads. Zia sat quietly, nervous.

"Mr. Yazzie," the dean began. "What made you come up with a concept that combines teaching the basics along with teaching jewelry making, rug weaving—and then selling the work to the public?"

"I wanted to combine theory, practice and tradition. Honestly, the Navajo children don't always excel in school. It's so foreign, and they don't get a lot of support from their elders. So I thought if we could combine the traditional learning of the arts and crafts with the basic format of formal education maybe there would be more interest...more success."

The department chair looked perplexed. "Are you serious about this concept or is it just what you need to meet the requirements for your degree?"

"Oh. I'm very serious. I've thought about this for a long time. You see, where I grew up, anyone with a G.E.D. could teach at our school. It shouldn't be that way. But it's more than just good teachers and curriculum. The concept has to include Navajo tradition in order to be successful."

"Well, I think it's brilliant," Dr. Ortiz chimed, "Especially the way you integrated the retail concept to help support the school and even reward the students for their work. How did you come up with that?"

"I've been working for an Indian arts and crafts store in Gallup. Seeing the business from the money-making perspective gave me the idea. Why can't we make more of that money ourselves and have it benefit the Navajo community? It's about gaining knowledge and also rewarding tradition."

The dean took his glasses off and rubbed his eyes. "Mr. Yazzie, I think we need to go over a few things here and see if we can approve this project as an independent study. If you would step out into the hallway, we'll discuss this and call you in with our decision."

"Yes, sir."

Zia paced. He sat. He waited. The longer he sat there, the more doubtful he became. He would be stuck working for Ben and never get his degree.

About five minutes after eleven, Dr. Ortiz opened the door and motioned him into the conference room.

"Mr. Yazzie," the dean said. "We have approved your independent study. You have a lot of work to do to develop this concept, and we expect clear and concise curriculum plans and study outlines to be presented to this committee every two weeks throughout the semester."

Zia exhaled in relief.

"Yes, sir, I understand."

"I'm very excited about your Navajo Arts and Crafts Academy," Dr. Ortiz crooned.

"Oh, Ramona, you're such an idealist," the dean said. "I like the idea too, but I don't see how it can ever become a reality. It's a little outrageous."

"We have benefactors you know," the department chair added.

Ramona Ortiz stood up with a start. "Oh, that reminds me, Zia, I have your scholarship and registration documents here."

She handed him the paperwork and told him to take it to the cashier's office to officially register.

"Thank you very much, Dr. Ortiz," he said taking the documents from her.

Zia felt satisfied and relieved. He had his approval and his scholarship and a lot of work ahead of him.

He thanked the committee and shook hands with each of them. They scheduled their next meeting and outlined their expectations.

When he left, he realized it was already 11:20. He had just enough time to race across campus to the Frontier. He would go to the cashier's office later.

The restaurant was a large place always full of students studying, lazing around, drinking coffee and eating their famous cinnamon rolls.

Zia darted through the door and scanned the restaurant for Selene. No Selene. Oh well, he shrugged.

Behind him came a tap on his shoulder.

"Hey, Gallup guy, long time no look," sounding like a Navajo girl.

He turned to see Selene grinning.

Selene and Zia sat across from each other in the crowded restaurant, each enjoying a bowl of meaty green chile and a tortilla.

"So, Zia, give me three good reasons why I should get my degree in education."

Selene took a small piece of tortilla and scooped up a dollop of green chile and took a bite.

"I don't know you well enough to give you three good reasons. I can only speak for myself, because I want to give Navajos a better education."

"You know, this may sound strange, but you're not like other Navajos."

"That's probably because I'm half Navajo."

"Well, I'm half Spanish."

"Pretty good alright," Zia said, sounding like a Navajo.

"*Está bien*," Selene answered.

They both chuckled and agreed to meet there again in exactly two weeks for further discussion.

"I have a lot of questions for you, Zia."

"With as many questions as you ask, you seem more like a reporter. Maybe you should change your major to journalism if you want more excitement."

She stared at him almost stunned.

"Ay Dios. I think you might be right!"

Zia paid their check and they walked out into the crisp, clear January afternoon.

"Thanks, Zia…So, I'll see you in two weeks?" she asked, then winked.

Imitating a Navajo accent and skewed expression, he said, "If you don't show up then, you'll shore hurt my feelers."

They both laughed and headed in opposite directions. Zia looked back at her as he crossed the street heading into campus again. He liked the bounce in her step and the way her long hair swung freely as she strolled in the other direction. He hoped she would show up in two weeks.

Zia hurried across campus to register then drove to the mall to check out the Indian arts and crafts store there as well as the fine jewelry stores, then headed back to Gallup. He felt accountable and protective of the store—and then there was all the work to do on his independent study. Responsibility weighed heavily on him.

***

Louise tuned in to the conversation Karen and Jerry were having. Zia told her to keep an eye on them, and she wanted to give him the full report when he returned. Besides, she was anxious to hear if his proposal was accepted.

Earlier, after she opened the store, unlocked the vault, got the cash bag, put the $200 in the cash register and set the cash bag with yesterday's receipts and monies for the deposit on her desk, she locked the vault—just in case. Then she put the cash bag in the top desk drawer and closed the office door behind her as she walked out to spy on her two co-workers.

"I still think we should get commission for our sales. Ooowee, would I be outselling you then, Karen."

"Oh, you think? You haven't seen what I can do. I'm a very

persuading person."

She flipped her curls back and planted her hands on her hips.

"Yeah, I know you're sitting on a gold mine, Karen. Catch my drift?"

"You pig. What's with you…it's like you're a woman hater or something."

Jerry took a drag on his cigarette.

"I don't give a rat's ass about women, Karen."

She walked toward him and wagged her index finger at his face.

"Jerry…"

"Children, children, here comes a customer," Louise scolded.

"Oops. Sorry, Louise. Jerry gets me so riled up."

Louise walked across the store and turned the radio down. They were always blasting that country music. Why couldn't they play some nice Elvis songs, she wondered? Oh well, those two are like oil and water.

She strolled to the office to prepare the deposit and the daily report of yesterday's sales.

Ben would be in Dallas for another day, and Zia would probably be back late this afternoon. She wanted everything in order.

***

Cecelia padded downstairs in her robe and slippers—needing coffee. She hadn't slept well. The same dream haunted her over and over—the one where her secret kept bubbling to the surface.

"Buenos dias, Luz. ¿Qué estás 'ciendo?"

"Nada, nada. Just you and me, CeCe," she told her while pouring

her a cup of coffee.

"Well. Luz, I don't know why, but I feel all icky and bloated and had bad dreams."

"Could be you're just containing water or having a urinal infection. Is it time for your cycle? Maybe you need a *curandera*."

"Luz, *por Dios santo*, you know I had my tubes tied after Selene was born."

"Pobrecita, I'm sorry…I guess I wanted to forget."

"You know, CeCe, I always hoped there would be a bunch of *niños* running around this house with noses full of *mocos* and smearing fingerprints all over everything so I could watch Señor Ben go *loquito*. He probably would've had a culinary."

Cecelia laughed so hard she nearly recovered from the doldrums.

"Dáme más café, Luz, por favor, before *I* have a *coronary* trying to picture that."

Cecelia poured cream into the coffee and stirred and stirred—distant.

I had my tubes tied, she thought, because I didn't want children of Ben's. They would look different than Selene and my deception would be revealed. I never told him, and I swore Luz to secrecy. That's probably why she forgot.

"CeCe, you're a million miles away. What are you thinking about?"

"Oh… ah…ah, I hope everything is going well for Selene. She seems to have lost her interest in becoming a teacher. She had a meeting with her counselor yesterday morning, so I hope she'll call later and fill me in. I don't want her to get discouraged and give up, and on top of it, she's living at the abuelita's house. I know it's close to campus, but she could be in a sorority with other girls her age. I shudder to think what she would say if I suggested *that* again."

"Selene has a lot of friends, CeCe, and she's a smart girl. She'll find out what she really wants to do and be back on her toes again in no time. Remember, it's what we hold in our hearts that makes us who we are."

Unfortunate, she thought, but true.

***

It didn't take long for Ben to convince O'Malley's Gems & Jewels that a line of handmade Indian jewelry would boost their sales. With seventy stores across the country—and one showcase in each store displaying and selling his wares—Ben Monroe was on a profit-making high.

Their head buyer, Michael Alexander, was scheduled to arrive in Gallup next week. Ben sized him up as a know-it-all, but he could handle him. He chuckled picturing Alexander showing up in his fancy suit and tie and wing-tip shoes—his leather briefcase at his side. He would stand out in Gallup.

As he boarded the plane, a sense of weariness overcame him. The adrenaline rush from his negotiations and deal-making had worn him out. He was tired. He slid into his seat, buckled up and closed his eyes. He looked forward to a quickie with Karen.

"Peace on earth," he always told her. "If all the world leaders had a tryst and a nap every day, there would be no more conflicts or wars."

Ben made sure he had his small spiral notebook and pen in the inside pocket of his jacket. He needed to make a to-do list for the store and for Zia. They had a lot to accomplish before Michael Alexander showed up.

***

The sun was rising earlier and soon the days would be longer. Zia anticipated spring and summer. He stepped out into the chilly morning to watch the rising sun reflect on the underside of the clouds where they held a peach glow.

He felt the weight of responsibility. With the work he had to produce on his independent study and non-stop whirlwind of projects at the store, he hadn't a minute to spare. Balance and harmony were required for him to meet the challenges and expectations that lay ahead. He closed his eyes and transported himself to the front door of his mother's hogan and recited the Navajo Blessing Way Prayer.

In beauty may I walk.
All day long may I walk.
Through the returning seasons may I walk.
On the trail marked with pollen may I walk.
With grasshoppers about my feet may I walk.
With dew about my feet may I walk.
With beauty may I walk.
With beauty before me, may I walk.
With beauty behind me, may I walk.

With beauty above me, may I walk.
With beauty below me, may I walk.
With beauty all around me, may I walk.
In old age wandering on a trail of beauty,
lively, may I walk.
In old age wandering on a trail of beauty,
living again, may I walk.
It is finished in beauty.
It is finished in beauty.

Zia inhaled a deep breath of cold air and walked to Boyd's. He felt his jacket pocket to make sure his small spiral notebook and pen were there—he needed to jot down ideas, notes and procedures for this first phase of his project due in two weeks. He had to use his free time wisely.

He also wanted to visit with his friends and roommates in Albuquerque—shoot some baskets, relax and laugh, have a few beers. It felt like he was turning into someone else. Ben Monroe.

Zia hurried and finished his atole and gulped the last of his coffee. Ben would be back from Dallas, and he wanted to get to the store early to make sure everything was in good order and talk over his merchandising ideas with Ben when he arrived. He lettered "lighting" in his notebook. The fine jewelry stores he visited yesterday had excellent lighting that made their diamonds sparkle. Silver and turquoise would glisten with improved lighting. He would bring that up when they met.

Louise, already in her office, looked up from her desk and waved at Zia. He smiled, feeling secure with Louise there in her trusted position.

Soon Ben zipped through the front door smiling. "I did it. O'Malley's Gems & Jewels is going to carry one showcase of Indian jewelry in each of their seventy stores."

"Congratulations," Zia said, giving Ben a hearty handshake.

"But it means work. Their buyer, Michael Alexander, will be here next Thursday. I was thinking that we could suggest a similar selection for each store and make him believe he's the one who did the choosing. He's a bit of a hot shot. We have so much to do...I don't think anybody can take their days off next week. Is that a problem, Zia?"

"Not at all, Ben. I don't have to be in Albuquerque until the following Thursday."

Zia would have to use his time wisely to work on his project. He couldn't afford to get behind.

"Ben, how are we going to coordinate seventy orders at once?"

"I thought that through on the plane yesterday. What I'll tell Alexander is that while he's here, we'll make the master selection. When he's satisfied with the assortment and the cost, we'll use that model to duplicate the remaining orders and prepare them for shipping. We might have to put in a few late nights to get it done."

"That sounds like a good plan," Zia agreed. "What about Jerry and Karen?"

"I'll talk to them when they come in. We need as much help as we can get. Besides, there's a bonus in it for them."

"Oh, that reminds me, Ben," Zia motioned him away from Louise's earshot. "The other day when I was finishing a big order, I noticed that we were missing a bag of Effie Calavaza bracelets from the vault. I asked Jerry and Karen, but they didn't know anything about it."

"Hmm. Something is going on here. I'm glad you caught that," Ben pondered, lighting another cigarette.

"Here comes our crew, we'll have to talk again later," Ben said, while he took another drag on his smoke.

Inside the squat adobe house close to the UNM campus, the abuelita—an amateur genealogist—bent over the dining room table, studying the family history charts and graphs that were spread out on the antique oak table with its carved rams' heads at the corners. That table had been in the Aragon family for over a century.

The keeper of the family tree and historical data, the abuelita had spent seemingly endless hours at the archives in Santa Fe copying old census information and studying rolls of microfiche containing birth certificates, baptisms and marriages—many documents hand-written in old Spanish script. The dizzying reels spinning by her 83-year-old eyes gave her vertigo, but she continued her quest. She also visited elderly relatives and recorded their oral histories—often uncovering the illegitimacies, the affairs and other secrets whispered to her over endless cups of Manzanilla tea.

According to the abuelita, the Aragons were isolated in the land-grant town of Cebolleta—sent there by the King of Spain in the early 1800s—and, from her research it seemed there was a lot of inter-marriage.

"*Válgame, Dios*, I swear the more investigating I do, the more I'm convinced I am my own cousin!" she would say throwing her hands in the air.

The abuelita insisted that everyone in her family speak Spanish, and she, herself, loved to speak the old Spanish of the Colorado Plateau—using the ancient vocabulary. Her mind was always a century away. Selene would often tease her about being frozen in time like a fossil.

Later, sitting together at the kitchen table for a dinner of *fideo* soup with its wholesome chicken, vegetables and vermicelli noodles, Selene discussed her desire to change her major.

"How about history, Selena?" She insisted on calling her Selena—not Selene.

"No, that's what *you* like, abuelita." Selene grinned then said, "Today I had lunch with a guy from Gallup. He told me I should be a journalist because I ask so many questions."

"*Somos las mismas.* But, of course, you're just like me, Selena."

"Anyway, he's working on some education project for the reservation so that he can graduate in May. He's half Navajo."

"Half Navajo?" The abuelita knitted her brows. "His people raided our ancestors in their village of Cebolleta and killed many of the children. You can't go around with Navajos."

"For God's sake, abuelita, that was more than a hundred years ago. It's 1974. Besides I'm not going around with him."

Although he is really cute and nice, she thought.

"Well, enough of that. I have an essay due in English tomorrow, and I have to go to the dorm and use Becky's typewriter. So I'll see you later."

Selene kissed her great-grandmother on the cheek, then grabbed her books, purse and down jacket and headed out the door. She should have taken English 102 last year, but she couldn't get the professor she wanted. Now she was determined to do all the work and get a good grade.

Her dad's old Lincoln—that she inherited when he bought the new one—sat in the driveway. She wished she had a spiffy red Mustang like her mom, but the big maroon tank would have to do for now. Maybe she should take it up to Española and have it converted into a low rider? She giggled to herself picturing the big Lincoln with hydraulics and fancy hub caps and a tiny chain steering wheel. The square body could shine in a sparkly fluorescent pistachio green or chartreuse with Our Lady of Guadalupe painted on the hood.

Before she backed out, she fumbled through her 8-track tapes— Joni Mitchell, Joan Baez and Linda Ronstadt. Then she popped in the Cat Stevens tape with her favorite song—"Moonshadow." She cranked up the sound and sang along. That was *her* song.

Her thoughts jumped to Zia Yazzie. Maybe it's that he's not a beer-slugging, ass-grabbing frat boy. I'm so sick of them. There's something about him I like.

***

The store was buzzing with energy while the crew organized the merchandise for Michael Alexander's arrival the following day. Ben insisted on a systematic and well-organized vault where rings, earrings, pendants and bracelets were displayed in black velvet-lined jewelry trays or gift boxes and lined up along the counter above the storage cabinets and arranged neatly on the table in the center of the vault. Squash blossom necklaces, concho belts, bolo ties, heishi, fetishes and liquid silver hung from the black painted peg board that lined the walls. Bright fluorescent lights and everyone busy with silver polishing cloths made the merchandise glisten.

Zia noticed that even Karen and Jerry were getting along. But, of course, Ben hovered so closely that no snide remarks spilled from either of them. About three hours into the mission, Karen whined, "Do we get to have lunch?"

"Sure," Ben shrugged. We can get some sandwiches at the Route 66 Café."

"I can pick up the sandwiches, Ben," Jerry offered.

Zia continued to put chains on pendants and place each in an individual gift box left open for display.

"It's twelve o'clock, Zia, aren't you hungry?" Karen quizzed.

Zia looked up from his work.

"I'm Navajo, Karen, I don't need the clock to tell me when to eat."

Ben cracked a smile.

"But I will have a ham and cheese on rye."

"Funny, I didn't think Navajos ate ham and cheese on rye," Karen volleyed.

"Well, I guess there's always a first time. Or maybe I should have a Navajo specialty—a bologna and cheese on white bread."

"Or Spam," added Jerry.

"Yeah, Spam—especially fried. Mmm."

"Enough of the hamming it up," Ben joked. "Jerry, you go get sandwiches for yourself, Zia and Louise. Karen is coming with me. Ben reached into his pocket and pulled out a fat wad of money and handed him a couple of twenties.

Jerry glanced back at Zia and rolled his eyes like he knew what Ben was having for lunch.

After their sandwich break, Zia suggested Jerry watch the store and wait on customers while he finished merchandising the vault.

"That way, Jerry, by the time Ben and Karen get back from lunch, we should be ready for Michael Alexander."

"Lunch, my ass," Jerry snickered.

It was nearly 2 p.m. when Ben and Karen returned. A bit rumpled, Karen grabbed her purse from the shelf under the cash register and headed for the restroom. Ben went straight to the office to talk to Louise, avoiding eye contact with Jerry. Zia stayed in the vault.

By closing time, the store was ready. Michael Alexander would fly into Albuquerque, rent a car and arrive at the store around 11:00 a.m. They were ready for him.

***

Karen dressed in a black polyester jump suit and pinned her hair up in a French twist with a few curls cascading alongside her face, showing off the large dangling turquoise earrings that matched her squash blossom and thick cuff bracelet. She slipped the concho belt around her hips, cinched it closed and wiggled it into place. Checking for plenty of cleavage, she gave herself one last approving look in the mirror to make sure her makeup was perfect then blew herself a big Marilyn Monroe kiss—and dabbed an extra drop of Jungle Gardenia behind her ears.

She wanted to look her best, because Ben would probably invite this Michael Alexander person to dinner, and surely she would join them.

Everyone was at the store early to go over the procedures for the morning and check final details. Ben seemed a little nervous and preoccupied, Karen thought.

"My, my Christmas," Jerry hissed. "Aren't we looking scandalous this morning?"

Karen shot him a searing look and wiggled away.

Louise was on the phone ordering a platter of sandwiches to be delivered around noon, and she had stocked the small refrigerator in her office with Cokes and Tab.

About an hour later the tall handsome buyer from O'Malley's Gems & Jewels glided through the door in a tailored suit, an air of self-importance and a practiced smile. Ben marched over and offered a strong handshake.

"Good to see you, Michael. How was your trip?"

"The flight was fine, but that was one boring drive from Albuquerque to *this* place."

Ben seemed to ignore his haughtiness and motioned him toward Zia and Louise to begin introductions.

"Christmas," Jerry whispered. "Quit staring."

Then, there he was in front of them.

"Jerry, Karen, I'd like you to meet Michael Alexander."

He shook Jerry's hand in passing, and gave Karen a lengthy handshake and a hot look up and down.

Karen appeared to melt.

This might be an interesting day after all, she thought.

"Okay, let's get to work," Ben said, giving Karen a hard look. She noticed his tight jaw and white lips.

"Jerry and Karen, you man the store, while Zia and I work with Michael in the vault."

They both stopped in their tracks and looked at Zia for a clue. He shrugged.

"Jerry, you creep, we're being tossed aside. Ben probably heard what you said to me."

"He didn't have to hear a thing, Christmas. Ben saw you salivating over Mr. Hot Shot, and he's pissed."

"Well, he'll just have to get over it."

Karen sulked and slumped against the showcase next to the cash register. What was happening? Her gut was telling her something…like a bad feeling that her scheme was about to unravel. She wondered if she might lose at her own game. It was that cold look on Ben's face that rattled her.

What? Suddenly I'm supposed to be faithful to an older married guy who is just using me? But I'm using him, too—in more ways than he realizes, she thought.

Sure, she liked the perks—the car, the apartment, the jewelry, the cash. She knew she had better play her cards right—or plan to leave. She realized exactly what her gut was telling her. Leave. Run away.

Jerry paced and smoked—ignoring his surroundings.

Karen opened the cash register and pulled out all the bills except the ones, rolled up the chunk of money, shoved it in her purse and walked out.

No more of that "peace on earth" bullshit, she thought. Oh baby, Oh baby. I'm out of here.

Jerry turned when he heard the door open, thinking it was a customer and saw Karen stomping out.

He sauntered over to the showcase by the cash register. The cash drawer lay wide open and emptied out—except for the ones.

What is she up to…what got into her undies? Jerry wondered.

Jerry slipped past the vault door and into the office.

"Louise," he said nervously. "Karen just took a bunch of cash out of the register and split."

Louise leaned forward, surprised.

"What? Why would she do a stupid thing like that?"

"I was having a smoke over by the Navajo rugs, and when I turned around I saw her leaving. Then I went over by the register and saw that the drawer was open. She took everything but the ones. What the hell am I supposed to do? Should I tell Ben?"

"Not now. Let me think."

Louise leaned back in her chair and sat there stunned for the moment.

"What got into her?"

"I think it was that Michael Alexander? Did you see how she looked at him?"

"Oh, yes. And I saw the look on Ben's face, too. Oh boy, of all days," Louise said.

Louise opened the bottom drawer of her desk and took out a cash box.

"Okay, I'll give you some money from petty cash so you have change for the drawer, but I don't think we should say anything to Ben yet."

Louise sat back as if pondering a scenario that would work for today.

"If Ben asks, I'll tell him that I sent Karen home because she was sick. I don't want him to get upset or embarrassed with Michael Alexander here. The O'Malley's Gems & Jewels sale means too much to him. Besides, she'll probably get over her little snit and come back before the day is out, and Ben won't even know what happened."

Jerry noticed someone stepping into the store. "Oh, Louise, it looks like your sandwiches are here."

"Okay, I'll take the sandwiches into the vault. I have some paper plates and napkins set up already, and I'll get them some sodas. If we can keep them in there as long as possible, maybe Ben won't notice that Karen is gone."

Louise stepped out of the vault with a plate of sandwiches for her and Jerry to share and reported that everything seemed to be going well.

"Ben and Zia have Michael Alexander at their advantage. I'd say they'll be done with the master selection in a couple of hours. Whew, then we really have to work."

"Yeah, and no Karen. What a wench," Jerry snapped.

Meanwhile, Karen had changed into jeans, a sweatshirt and Keds and scurried through the apartment gathering her clothes, make-up, jewelry and few other belongings and stuffed everything into her car. Ben would know she was gone when he saw the apartment. He paid the rent, so she just left—no note, no explanation—just gone.

With an in-your-face grin, she dropped the bag of Effie Calavaza bracelets on the kitchen counter. They were of no use to her now.

Before she disappeared, Karen went to the bank and closed her checking account. She had enough cash to last for several months with the money she had stolen right in front of their faces.

Dumb like a fox. Louise should have figured it out, she thought.

On those small sales—a few rings, earrings or pendants—she would ask the customer, "Is that cash, check or credit card?" If they used a credit card, she would add the total on the small calculator beside the register, then she would imprint the credit card on the triplicate credit card sales slip and write in the total sale and sales tax. She would call the 800 number for an approval code when necessary and give a copy to the purchaser. Her brilliance was that she never rang it into the register. When no one was looking, she cashed her credit card slip out of the drawer. When Louise or Zia checked out at the end of the day, the total on the z-tape matched the total cash and credit card slips in the drawer. Her scheme counted on a good number of cash sales to make it work.

She raced onto I-40 and headed west, and flipped her finger out the open car window. "See you, sucker. Hollywood, here I come!"

**

It was late afternoon, when Michael Alexander left for Albuquerque, and Ben breathed a huge sigh of relief and pride. "We did it, Zia. Now the work begins. My only concern is that they pay as planned—30, 60, 90."

"How does that work, Ben?"

"The deal was they pay 1/3 of the total invoices in 30 days, 1/3 in 60 days and the rest in 90 days. It's a negotiating tactic that benefits their cash flow. I had to give in to it. We're still doubling our money. I just hope they sell the merchandise quickly, and we can keep re-stocking. Speaking of inventory, we're going to wipe this place out."

"Okay, let's get started," Ben clapped. "I'll get Jerry and Karen in here to help."

Louise was standing at the vault door and motioned for Ben to come into the office, then nervously told him about Karen. He was silent.

Ben's jaw tightened up in anger, and his lips turned white. He smashed his cigarette into the ash tray on Louise's desk and stormed out of the store.

"Oooowee, I wouldn't want to be *her* right now," Jerry whistled.

Zia stepped out of the vault looking confused. "What's going on, Jerry?"

When Jerry set the scene, Zia shook his head. "Of all days."

"Well, I'm going to go *hide* in the vault and get to work. Do you want to help, Jerry?"

"Yup, I guess so."

They walked toward the vault, Zia asked Louise to watch the store while they started assembling the orders.

"Jerry, do you think Ben's mad about the money or about Karen?" Zia asked.

"Shoot, it's about her. She smacked his ego around and then walked out like the wench that she is. The money she took from the drawer is pocket change to Ben. That girl needs to mend her ways, or before she knows it, she'll be long in the tooth and bartending at the VFW."

Ben zoomed over to the apartment and banged on the door. No answer. He unlocked it and stepped into near emptiness. He had rented it furnished, but it was apparent that Karen and her belongings were gone—only the sickeningly sweet scent of her perfume remained. He walked toward the kitchen and saw the bag of Effie Calavaza bracelets sitting on the counter.

He slammed the door and walked to his car trying to figure out what she was up to.

It had to be more than just a Michael Alexander attraction, he thought.

Suddenly Ben got it. Somehow, she had given herself away and lost her disguise. Her dishonesty bared itself right before my eyes, he thought. Has she been using me all along? Probably. But what else? What else was she stealing?

Ben was mad as hell. The more he thought about Karen, the angrier he got. He drove back to the store and made a beeline for Louise's office and slammed the door. Louise was getting ready to leave for the day and fell back into her chair.

"There's more to this, Louise. I think Karen was up to something. I want an audit of the daily reports and z-tapes to see if she was stealing more than this sack of Effie bracelets."

"But, we were never short, Ben. Every day the drawer matched the total sales."

"Something doesn't add up. Pull out an envelope from a day when Karen worked and let me look at it."

Louise went to the file cabinet where the manila daily report envelopes were lined up. She pulled out the past Saturday. There were always a lot of sales, and everyone was on the floor.

Ben sat and looked through the z-tape. There weren't any entries where a sale would be credited back as a return. There were a few times when the cash tend key had been pressed to open the drawer— for what reason, he wondered. Then he went through the store copies of credit card sales slips that were imprinted by placing the credit card in the slot and sliding the imprinter over the triplicate slip. The imprint of the credit card and the store's information appeared on each copy with the magic of carbon paper—the hard copy went into the bank deposit, the customer got a copy, and the store got a copy. He went through them and matched up each credit card slip with a sale—however, several of Karen's weren't on the z-tape. That seemed odd.

Then it hit him. The customer wouldn't know if she didn't ring it up. They had their credit card receipt.

"Louise, what if she tracked the cash sales?" Ben said. He jumped out of his chair and paced. "I get it!" He slammed his hand on the desk. "She didn't ring up the credit card sales...just put the receipts in the drawer and took the cash. Bingo!"

"Wow, that's devious," Louise said shocked.

"Okay, this is what I want you to do—not tonight, but tomorrow. Go through the daily report envelopes and identify all the credit card sales of Karen's that don't show up on the z-tape, and give me a total. I don't want anyone to know what you're doing. They'll be busy enough trying to get the orders out."

Ben left the office, and stepped into the vault to see the progress being made on the orders. Zia and Jerry were working diligently.

"You guys can quit for the night. Today was just too chaotic for me to be able to help you now."

"Jerry can leave, if he wants," Zia said. "But I'm going to keep at it as long as I can."

"Well, that's up to you. I've had it," said a disgusted Ben. "I'm going home."

***

"What is Ben so angry about, Luz?" Cecelia asked as she sipped her morning coffee."

"I have no idea, CeCe. Ignorance is *blitz*."

"I thought he would be on cloud nine with that huge sale to that jewelry chain, but he is just mean and nasty. I don't want to be anywhere around him, Luz."

"When he came downstairs this morning, CeCe, he was in a huff. Even his aura was dark."

Cecelia rolled her eyes, though she was used to Luz's mystical insights.

"Maybe he is just under a lot of stress trying to get all those orders together. Should I offer to help? I think I'll stop by the store this morning and talk to Louise."

"I don't know, CeCe. He's fixed in his ways and doesn't like interference. Maybe you should call Louise and see what she says."

Louise was tactful.

"We have it under control, Cecelia. Don't worry. He'll be back to his old self in a few days."

Yeah, right, Louise thought.

She had come in early to audit the z-tapes and saw that Zia had been there all night and looked exhausted. Boxes full of jewelry sat scattered around the vault—invoices with adding machine tapes stapled to them rested on top of each.

"You better go home and get some rest, young man. You look awful."

"I thought I could keep going, but I need a nap and a shower and a whole pot of coffee. I hope Ben doesn't mind if I'm gone for a couple of hours."

"Don't worry, when he sees all those boxes ready to go, he's going to be happy."

Louise escorted Zia to the door and locked it behind him and got to work deciphering the z-tapes—and it wasn't pretty. Karen had gotten to Ben for a bundle. It had never occurred to Louise to go through the tapes in that way.

Well, that Ben is one clever man, Louise thought.

Ben showed up a few minutes later and stood in front of the vault, surprised to see all the boxes of jewelry and invoices ready to go.

"I just sent Zia home for a while. He looked exhausted," Louise called out from the office.

"Well, I'm impressed," Ben sighed.

"That is one special young man. Where did you ever find him?"

Ben didn't answer and walked into the office to see the stack of daily report envelopes on Louise's desk.

"Any pattern evolving here, Louise?"

"Unfortunately, yes. I'm writing down the dates and the totals, and it's a lot of money.

"Okay, the other thing I need is the license plate number for the Mustang. We have that file here, don't we?"

"Sure, I can get it right now." Louise got up and headed for the file cabinet. She handed Ben the folder with the title, registration and license information.

She didn't dare ask what he was going to do. He set the file on his desk next to the phone.

"Let me know when you've finished and have a total, I'll be back later."

Ben walked past the cash register and abruptly turned around back toward the office.

"Another thing, Louise," he called out, gesturing with his index finger in the air. "Since, Zia's not here right now, will you get the register ready for today's business? I want you to put an extra $20 in the drawer." Then he turned and left.

I get it, Louise thought. He doesn't trust *anyone*. When Zia checks out tonight, he'd better be $20 over. If not, Ben will know he pocketed it. And I'll keep an eye on Jerry. I don't want that drawer opened unless it's for a sale.

Louise readied the cash register and turned on the lights and unlocked the front door. Soon Jerry, exhaling the smoke from the cigarette he had flicked onto the sidewalk, stepped into the store.

"Mornin', Louise. Any word from the wench?"

Louise just shrugged and shook her head no.

"Where's Zia?"

"He was here all night, so he went home for a nap. Take a look in the vault."

Jerry whistled when he saw the array of boxes—a whistle that told Louise he was glad the worst was over.

***

Zia shook himself awake, accompanied by a dull headache that reminded him of all-nighters during final exam week. He forced himself out of bed and stood under the hot shower longer than usual and dressed quickly. Grabbing his jacket, he slipped it on as he walked into the crisp February morning. Sunrise had eluded him from the belly of the vault. He needed food and coffee.

"You're late," chirped Betty as he slid into the usual booth at Boyd's. She poured him a big mug of coffee, and he hoped with a few more cups, his sluggishness would fade. He ordered atole, knowing a big meal might knock him out. Besides, he couldn't choke down another sandwich.

By the time he arrived at the store, Jerry was strolling around with a smoke and whistling to the country tune on the radio, while a couple of buyers were hovered over a few trays of rings, piling up their choices on the showcase glass. He should be watching those people, Zia thought. They could just slip a few rings in their pockets while he's not looking.

Zia went behind the showcase and greeted the people and asked if they were finding a good selection. "We have a ring mandrel so you can check sizes—6 is the most common for women." Jerry took the hint, put out his smoke and grabbed the steel ring-sizing dowel from under the showcase and slid one of the rings onto it. "Size 5 on this one. If you want, I have a jewelry mallet that I can easily tap the shank and stretch the silver to make it into a size 6?"

Walking into the vault, Zia exhaled a giant sigh knowing the work still ahead of him. He didn't think he would be stuck with this job alone—but that's the way it was turning out. He peeled off his jacket and rolled up his sleeves and started packing. Double-check these invoices he told himself. As fatigued as he became last night, he could have easily missed something. Get it done. Get it done, he told himself. Hanging over him was another section of his independent study which was due next Thursday—he hadn't worked on it in days.

Zia listened to Jerry chumming it up with his buyers. It turned out that they were from Cleveland where they owned a Hallmark store and wanted to put in a case of Indian jewelry.

"We flew to Phoenix and rented a car," the man who called himself Hank said. That place is nice this time of year. The weather is sunny and then there are the restaurants and beautiful hotels and golf courses."

"But the thing I noticed were all the Mexicans working everywhere," his wife added. "Are those people illegal?"

"No doubt," Jerry piped up. "Heck, they ought to just get rid of them and send them back to Mexico and let the colored people do those jobs."

Jerry's bigotry infuriated Zia—most of the time he ignored him. But not today. Instead, he stomped out of the vault and stood with his hands on his hips. "Hey, Jerry, you know there's always been illegal immigration. We Indians used to call it 'the White man.'"

The three of them stood speechless. Zia returned to the vault with an adrenaline rush that energized him for his task, and Jerry continued his selling—more professionally.

By the time Ben showed up with his arms loaded with sacks of jewelry, Jerry was writing the invoice for his buyers and Zia had packed several boxes ready for shipping. Ben gave Jerry an approving nod and stopped at the vault to see the progress.

"Good job, Zia. That's a lot of work you got stuck with."

He placed the sacks of jewelry on the table in the vault. "Zia, I appreciate your hard work."

"Thanks, Ben."

"I drove down to Zuni this morning. We needed to replace some of this inventory, and frankly, I needed some time to think. I've made a lot of mistakes in my life," his voice trailed off.

"Like me?" Zia lowered his eyes.

"What! You weren't a mistake. An accident maybe," he mumbled. "But without accidents a lot of people would never have children. Zia, you are my only son. Do you hear me—my only son— and you make me proud."

"Then why am I a secret?"

"That's a mistake," Ben sighed. "And I have to figure a way to change it, because secrets turn into lies."

Ben took a deep breath, turned and walked out of the vault and into the office and shut the door.

"What's the verdict, Louise?"

She handed him the yellow legal pad with dates and amounts.

"That bitch! My gut told me someone was stealing, but I couldn't figure out how. Look at this, she got more and more brazen as time went on. You know something...thieves always bury themselves, and she's not getting away with this."

Ben ripped the pages from the legal pad, stomped over to his desk and placed the yellow sheets in the Mustang's file folder.

"Louise, I'm going to pay a visit to my friend, the Chief of Police."

"That sleazy little bitch," he whispered as he walked out.

An hour or so later, Ben returned. He walked into the office, shut the door and took a folded paper from his jacket pocket.

"This is the police report, Louise. Put it in her payroll file. No one else is to know about this. I charged her with car theft and embezzlement, and I told the police she has drugs on her, too. I know they won't find drugs, but it seemed to pique their interest. I want her found. I told them she probably headed to California. They'll put out an APB."

Louise unfolded the police report and placed it in Karen's file. "What about all of her jewelry?"

"No, I gave her that jewelry, but if they find her and she has merchandise from the store, you bet I'll get that back."

Ben took a cigarette from the pack in his shirt pocket and felt for the silver and turquoise lighter in his pants' pocket, lit the cigarette, took a long drag.

"What a mistake. Louise, I don't want to talk about this again," and he marched out of the office to the vault door.

"Zia, why don't you check out the register a little early and go home? I'll help you finish this tomorrow morning, and we can take all the boxes to the post office. You look tired."

Ben walked past the showcases toward the cash register where Jerry stood. "How much did you end up selling those people this morning?"

Jerry pulled out the invoice with the check attached and handed it to Ben.

"Keep up the good work, and you shall be rewarded."

"Think commission, Ben."

"I'm thinking, I'm thinking." Ben said as he walked out the door.

Zia slipped behind the register and turned the key to the "z" function, and while the tale of the tape cranked out with the day's transactions, he stacked up the checks, credit card slips and cash, leaving $200 aside for the change in the drawer. Then, as usual, he added the stack to make sure it balanced with the total on the z-tape—he added it twice.

He scooped up the stack of receipts, the cash and z-tape, and walked straight to the office. "Louise, I must be too tired to add. Will you check this for me? I keep coming up $20 over."

God bless you, Zia, Louise thought.

When Zia left the store, he trudged along with his head down and his hands buried in the pockets of his jacket. Ben's words were ringing in his ears: "Zia, you are my only son."

***

Ben sank into the Lincoln and automatically put the key in the ignition. With the car idling, he sat there and stared, thinking. Son of a bitch, I've had it. First Karen screws me over and embezzles then

Zia wants to know why he's a secret. Shit! He pounded the steering wheel in frustration. I'm not supposed to have these kinds of problems. I just want to make money.

He massaged his forehead, hoped the headache would go away, put the car in gear and drove home. He lit a cigarette, and took one puff then threw it away. There was nowhere else to go but home. No more trysts with Karen—that sleazy, thieving bitch. No place but home.

He opened the door to the heavenly aroma of paella. Wow, his favorite.

Oh no. Now what...is it a birthday or anniversary that I've forgotten, he thought.

Cecelia turned and smiled a big hello as she placed the lengths of roasted red bell peppers across the top of the finished dish in her large round paella pan. It was her specialty—delicious and elegant—paella was always a hit. He stared at the saffron-yellow rice, the chicken and seafood dotted with green peas and topped with the strips of peppers. Suddenly he felt hungry.

"I thought we could celebrate your jewelry deal, Ben. Sit down in the dining room. Luz has the table set, and she'll pour you a glass of the Spanish wine that I've been saving for a special occasion."

"Well, this is a nice surprise." And he meant it. Ben sat in his chair at the head of the table and sipped red wine while Cecelia and Luz brought the paella, hard rolls and a crisp tossed salad to the table.

Ben relaxed and all tension drained out of him with the

wonderful meal, a few glasses of red wine and positive conversation about the deal with O'Malley's.

"So, what will you do next, Ben?"

He leaned back and took another sip of wine.

"What I've been thinking about is setting up a jewelry production operation where Navajo silversmiths could make a specific line of jewelry. That would be good for the mass-merchandising and profitability as well. Stores can't always order specific items, because we don't necessarily have a lot of the same things available all the time."

"That's exciting, Ben."

"Thanks, Cecelia, it's still in the idea stage, but I'm getting more serious about it."

"I'd like to help out if I could…for now, though, how about some flan and coffee, Ben?"

"That sounds fabulous."

"There goes the phone," Luz lamented and hurried toward the wall phone in the kitchen.

"Señor Ben, it's for you."

Ben strolled to the kitchen to take the call. When he hung up his thoughts relived the conversation with Officer Collins of the Flagstaff Police Department who had told him that they had arrested a Karen Johnson for car theft and embezzlement, but didn't find any drugs on her. She was staying at Little America, and another officer saw the Mustang with New Mexico plates and found her in the bar.

Officer Collins had asked if he wanted to press charges, but Ben told him that he would come to Flagstaff in the morning to go over everything. They would keep her in custody.

As he walked back into the dining room, thinking of Karen sitting in a jail cell overnight gave him satisfaction. Then he stopped short. How was he going to get the car back to Gallup? He'd call Louise and see if Fred could drive over with him and bring the car back. Then what would he do with the car? He could give it to Selene. She was still driving the old Lincoln.

"Well, it looks like I have to go to Flagstaff tomorrow," he was thinking fast. "I've been on the lookout for a slightly used Mustang for Selene, and I just got the call. I think I'll take Fred along with me to drive it back."

"How nice, Ben. Selene will be thrilled. She's been driving that huge Lincoln for too long."

"Now I can enjoy my flan," Ben smiled. Whew, if Cecelia had known what was going on with Karen, she would have thrown that flan in my face, he thought.

While Cecelia was helping Luz clear dishes, he went to the den and called Louise and made arrangements to pick up Fred before 9 a.m. and head to Flagstaff.

Then Ben stuck his head around the entrance to the kitchen. "Cecelia, I think I'll build a fire. Would you join me in the living room for a brandy?"

"So is Mr. Workaholic going to relax tonight?"

"Yes, thanks to you, dear, it's been a wonderful evening. How about we continue it upstairs?"

***

Karen sat in the jail cell sniveling—re-living her arrest. How could this have happened to her? She paced the floor whimpering. What to do? What to do?

A couple of drunk sorority girls from NAU were in the next cell, sleeping it off—waiting for daddy's credit card to bail them out. But she had no daddy with a credit card. Nobody was going to bail her out. She was told Ben Monroe would be there tomorrow to press charges. Then there would be a hearing and arraignment. Karen was looking at 3 to 5 years.

She glanced at herself in the aluminum foil mirror and could barely see her image—except for the black streaks of eyeliner and mascara that had run down her cheeks. She wet a rough paper towel and dabbed them away. She looked terrible. The orange prisoner uniform made her skin take on a yellow tinge. She sank down on the floor and stared at the bare walls for hour after hour. It was early morning when a guard brought her a vile breakfast. It was inedible, and she refused it, knowing she would vomit from the smell alone.

She lay on the cot and stared at the ceiling. Hours passed. Around 2 p.m., Officer Collins announced himself and came into her cell.

"Miss Johnson, I have spent the last few hours going over your case with Mr. Monroe. He examined your personal belongings and went through all the cash and your check book deposits and inspected the stolen car."

Karen looked up at the policeman with tears streaming down her face.

"Based on the car and the embezzled cash that Mr. Monroe reclaimed, he has decided not to press charges and left you $1,000 to start your life over... anywhere you want except Gallup, New Mexico."

She sobbed in disbelief.

"You are one lucky young lady. People as forgiving and generous as Mr. Monroe are rare. We will process your paperwork, and you will be free to go. Your belongings have been transferred to the compound, and you will be responsible to remove them within 48 hours or they will be donated to charity."

Karen was shaking—pale.

"Miss Johnson, hopefully you can start your life over. If you plan to stay in Flagstaff, we can refer you to some social services and counseling."

She just stood there with a blank stare.

***

His father's words—"Zia, you're my only son," kept ringing in Zia's ears as he strolled toward Boyd's for an early breakfast armed with the outline and notes for the next portion of his independent study which was due next week. He had slept for nearly 12 hours and felt revived. He was set to meet Ben at the store and haul all the boxes to the post office for mailing.

As soon as Betty saw him coming through the door, she poured him a mug of coffee. "Zia, our special today is huevos rancheros—red chile, frijoles, eggs and a tortilla."

"That sounds delicious, Betty. I'm hungry."

"Okay then, coming right up. Eggs over medium?"

"Perfect."

Zia drank more coffee and studied his outline, finding it hard to concentrate—thinking about being Ben's only son. But turning his concept into a reality presented a challenge. He had to be clear and concise and make the concept come alive.

After breakfast, he shoved all the notes into a big manila envelope and walked to the store.

Louise told him that Ben had to make an unexpected trip to Flagstaff, so if he and Jerry would load up the boxes in the store's pickup truck, she would give them the money for the mailings and watch the store while they were gone.

"I wonder if that Flagstaff trip has anything to do with the wench." Jerry said as he flicked his cigarette butt out the window of the pickup.

"I'm not even going to *try* and figure that out, Jerry. Who knows, maybe she's still in Gallup."

"You know what 'fat chance' means, buddy. She's not here. No way, Jose."

***

Over in Flagstaff—Ben in his own car and Fred in the Karen's Mustang—met at Little America for a late lunch. Then, they headed back to Gallup.

As he drove, Ben's mind wandered trying to find a solution to introducing Zia. His mother's old adage popped into his head, "What a tangled web we weave, when we practice to deceive."

Maybe I should practice the truth on Louise and witness her reaction to the news, he thought. They had been through a lot together lately—this might put her over the edge.

I hope they got the orders mailed to O'Malley's, he thought. I wish I could go to every one of those stores and make sure they're merchandised correctly—but I can't. That's Michael Alexander's territory. Sell, sell, sell. That's all I can hope for—and that they pay on time.

The long stretch of I-40 loomed. I just can't deal with the truth about Zia right now, he thought. It will have to wait a little longer.

He decided to have Cecelia drive the Mustang to Albuquerque and surprise Selene. Then she could bring the Lincoln back to Gallup.

Ben lit a cigarette and his thoughts shot back to business, money and planning his silversmith shop to create a new line of handmade Indian jewelry.

PART 3: DUAL WORLDS COLLIDE

Using every free minute, Zia completed the next section of his independent study and Louise produced a neatly typed copy. He drove along I-40 toward Albuquerque as the sun slipped above the horizon, and recited the Daybreak Song. Knowing he had plenty of time to arrive for his 10:00 a.m. meeting, he relaxed and took a deep breath. Besides, a day away from the intensity of the store would revive his spirit.

Zia smiled as he thought about Selene—wondering if she would show up at the Frontier. It had been two weeks, so she might have forgotten about him. He planned to wander over there for lunch anyway, and later get together with his roommates to play pool and have a few beers. He would stay at the apartment and head back to Gallup early the next morning in time to open the store.

***

Early morning snow dusted Albuquerque. From the kitchen window at the abuelita's house, Cecilia and Selene glanced at Sandia Peak blanketed in white while sitting at the small Formica table sipping coffee. The abuelita drank her cup of Manzanilla tea.

"What should we do today, Selene?"

"Well it's Thursday, and I don't have any classes. We could go shopping, go to a movie, or to lunch. Oh, lunch. You know, Mom, I'm supposed to meet Zia for lunch. You remember the guy I talked to at Boyd's that night we went to dinner?"

"Can't you call and reschedule?"

"Mom, I don't know how to get in touch with him. I'd hate to be rude and not show up. We're just meeting at the Frontier at 11:30. Come along. He's really nice. Then we can go to the mall."

Cecelia frowned and said she would stay with the abuelita while Selene went to lunch.

"Oh don't be such a dud. Zia is the one who told me I should be a journalist. He's very interesting. He's working on a special project to change the education system on the Navajo reservation—he's half

Navajo."

"So he's the one who got you thinking about journalism?"

"Yes, and I feel right about it. I sure didn't get the entrepreneurial gene from Dad, did I?"

Cecelia lowered her head. "No."

"Abuelita, do you want to go to lunch with us at the Frontier?"

"No, Selena, I'm too busy making a chart of all the intermarriages. I'm more convinced than ever that I am truly my own cousin. Ay Dios."

Selene and Cecelia chuckled.

"We'll be back after lunch to see if you want to do something with us this afternoon," Cecelia said dutifully.

"We can take my new car, Mom. It's stylin', I love it. And it's so much easier to park than the tank, although it reeks of some stinky sweet perfume. I'm going to have to air it out."

Selene found a parking spot along Central Avenue about a block away from the restaurant—and angled her new Mustang into a parallel parking place.

The Frontier buzzed with business as usual, and Selene spotted Zia standing near the check-out counter with a thick manila envelope in hand. She and her mother walked toward him, and he grinned when he saw them.

"Hi, Zia, I brought my mom along. She's here visiting."

Zia offered a hearty handshake. "Nice to meet you Mrs. ah—?

"—just call me 'Cecelia,'" she interrupted.

They sat at a small round table in the main dining room and each ordered green chile with beans and tortillas.

Selene asked Zia about his project, and he was pleased to say that things were going really well. He had to be back in two weeks with the next section. So he had a lot of work to do.

"Any *news* on your journalism career?"

"Actually, I've been thinking more seriously about it. I've talked to Dr. Ortiz and she is working on the curriculum with me. I can actually see myself as a news reporter."

"It's nice to hear you so encouraged, Selene," Cecelia said.

Just then, a nice looking middle-aged man with sandy-colored hair pulled back in a low ponytail stood next to the table. He was wearing a corduroy jacket with suede elbow patches, jeans and cowboy boots.

"Cecelia Aragon. Is that you?"

Cecelia looked shocked as she stared at the man.

"David Stanfield. What a surprise," she stammered. The color drained from her face.

"Uh…" Looking awkward, she turned, "Let me introduce you to my daughter, Selene, and this is her friend, Zia."

They each shook his hand and exchanged pleasantries.

"Selene looks exactly like you, Cecelia."

"Do you teach here at UNM?" Selene asked.

"Yes, and I'm chair of the journalism department and advisor to the student newspaper."

Selene gave Zia a wide-eyed look at that news.

"Selene, you seem so familiar. Have I met you before?

"No, I don't think so," she said, twisting a strand of hair around her finger.

David Stanfield shifted from one foot to the other, then popped the rubber band around the sheaf of paper he held.

"Sorry, I have to run," he said suddenly. Nice to see you again, Cecelia…and to meet you both," he said staring at Selene.

"Who was that, Mom?"

Cecelia took a deep breath. "David Stanfield. I used to date him while I was going to school here. He was a graduate student—a teaching assistant in English.

She fidgeted and ran her fingers through her long, dark hair and tucked one side behind her ear.

"That's when I lived with the abuelita—just like you do now— and…and she didn't like him because he was five years older than me and he wasn't Spanish. Actually, I think she put the *mal ojo* on him, too."

"That's our abuelita," Selene giggled.

Zia leaned over toward Selene and whispered. "What's the mal ojo?"

"The evil eye."

Zia nodded.

"What did Dad think?"

"I never told him about David Stanfield."

"You sure ask a lot of questions, Selene," Zia said as he grabbed the check for lunch. "You'll make a great reporter."

"No, no," said Cecelia, taking the check from Zia. "This is on me. I insist—anything to get this interrogation over."

They were all laughing as they scooted their chairs back.

Outside, Zia zipped up his jacket and thanked Cecelia and Selene for the enjoyable lunch.

"I'll be back in two weeks. Same time, same place."

"I'll try to make it," Selene said.

They waved and walked down the street and Zia watched them hop into a green Mustang that looked exactly like Karen's.

***

Cecelia faked aloofness about seeing David Stanfield. She regretted going to the Frontier with Selene. It had been almost 20 years since her affair with him. He'd left her feeling stupid and vulnerable. Today her nightmare stood right in front of her, and he had no idea that he was the father of her child. How could she continue this charade—she had lied to so many people.

Cecelia drifted into her own thoughts. Does David Stanfield deserve to know? Ben deserves to know. To make matters worse, what if Selene studies journalism and has David for an instructor or advisor? He's probably still single and preying on young students. God help us.

Cecelia wondered if Selene had inherited *his* love for the written word—*his* curiosity. It seemed apparent. She felt guilty that she had never given Ben Monroe children of his own, but she couldn't risk being exposed.

"Oh what a tangled web we weave, when we practice to

deceive." That Sir Walter Scott quote was one of David's favorites, she recalled. *Funny, I always thought it represented him—but it's me through and through. My life is a lie. That's probably why I'm so distant to Ben.*

Back at the abuelita's house, everything remained locked in time. Everything looked just as it had when Cecelia lived there when she attended UNM.

"Abuelita, do you want to go to a movie or go shopping at Winrock? Mom has to go back to Gallup tomorrow."

"*No, gracias.* The last time I went to a movie was *The Sound of Music* in 1965, and I don't need anything from a shopping center. I have all the clothes I need for the rest of my life."

"Well, at least go out to dinner with us after Selene and I go shopping. You need to get your mind off the shock of being your own cousin."

"How about Furr's Cafeteria?" the abuelita suggested.

"No way. Besides, everyone else who *is* their own cousin will probably be there," Selene joked.

"Instead we can just drive around arguing about where we should eat until we finally agree on a place—just like always," said Cecelia. "That's our tradition, isn't it?"

***

"Louise, do you think Fred would work here a few days a week for a while? I know he has problems with his legs, but he wouldn't have to stand all of the time. I can put a stool in the vault and he can sit and mark jewelry for us."

"I think he would enjoy it, Ben. I'll call him right now."

"Okay, tell him probably four days a week until Selene gets home for the summer. Then I'm going to get her in here whether she likes it or not. It's time she learns the business. I'll probably still need Fred to fill in for days off, though."

Zia and Jerry both showed up at the same time and quietly busied themselves getting the store open for business.

"Okay, guys," Ben said as he walked out of the office. "Louise's husband, Fred, is going to help us out for a while. He's coming in today for a few hours so you can show him the ropes."

Jerry shrugged and Zia said, "That's a good idea, Ben."

"Then, when my daughter gets back from UNM in May, I'm going to get her working in here, too. We'll be busier in the summer and need more help."

"Sounds good," Zia forced the comment.

So, Zia thought, he has a daughter in college. I wonder when he's planning on telling her about me.

When Ben walked into the vault, Jerry leaned over and gave Zia a slight elbow in the side.

"Hubba, Hubba, wait 'til you see her, Zia, you'll want to jump her bones."

Zia turned away and shuddered. Even to think anything inappropriate about his sister would cause Navajo taboo and require a Medicine Man to get rid of it.

Ben stepped out of the vault and motioned to Zia. "Will you

come into the office with me for a minute?"

"Bummer," Jerry whispered.

Ben closed the door and seemed nervous. He and Zia stood there silent for a minute, then Ben turned to Louise.

"Louise, there's something I want to tell you about Zia."

Louise leaned forward with an apprehensive look, her brows knitted.

"Zia is my son."

She gasped. "I wasn't expecting this at all. I don't know what to say," Louise said sinking back into her chair.

"The only people who know this are my parents and his mother and her family. Obviously she is Navajo. We fell in love the summer she worked in my father's trading post in Thoreau, then Zia..." his voice trailed off.

Zia just stood there. Silent.

"My wife and daughter don't know, and I'm wondering how to tell them and how they should meet. Frankly, I wanted to try it out on you first."

"Well, it's a shock. You know how much I think of Zia, but, I'm not in the same position as a wife or a sister." Louise took a deep breath. "If all this happened before you ever married, then I think they would understand. They might even be angry that you didn't bring him around sooner."

"You know me, Louise, I was just too busy trying to get ahead—working constantly—that the time just slipped away, I guess, and I just didn't know how to tell anyone."

Ben put his head down and sighed. I never imagined these two worlds would have occasion to come together, he thought.

"What do you think, Zia," Louise asked.

"I know I don't want to be a secret anymore."

"Okay… but for now no one else is to know. I have to tell my family first. This may take a little time. Whatever you do, don't tell Jerry. They would be furious if Jerry knew before they did."

Jerry continued to pace and smoke, wondering why everyone in the office looked so serious. Zia just stood there.

Louise got up from her desk and walked over and hugged Zia. "This is the best news I've heard in ages. Now, your being here makes sense to me." Tears welled up in her eyes.

Jerry stopped short and whispered. "What the hell is that about?"

When they left the office, Ben overheard Jerry asking Zia what had gone on in there.

"Jerry," Ben called out as he walked toward him. "Remember that commission we talked about? Well, I've decided to put it into effect immediately. I think it's important to reward hard work and enthusiasm to those who represent me."

"Zia, too?"

"Yes, Jerry. Zia, too."

***

Two weeks sped by for Zia. His level of concentration faltered a bit because he kept wondering when he would meet Ben's wife and his own half-sister. At least he knew he would appear out of the shadows soon. Now, Louise doted on him like a mother hen.

The next phase of his independent study was ready and he earned three days off for all the work he had put in on O'Malley's Gems & Jewels. The first day would be spent with his mother, the next in Albuquerque presenting his project—and hopefully Selene Aragon would show up at the Frontier. At least he finally knew her last name—not that it mattered, Navajos identify everyone by their clan.

Since he was staying in Albuquerque another day, he wanted to invite Selene to dinner or a movie, if he could get up the nerve.

Three days, he thought—it feels like a vacation.

He headed out early and drove to Thoreau. Canned goods and groceries filled the sacks on the passenger's seat of his pickup—things his mother would undoubtedly need.

Driving into Thoreau past Red Cliffs Trading Post, Zia wondered if he should ever stop and visit the strangers who were his grandparents. Probably not.

He felt at home, back in the arms of the red sandstone cliffs. His mother was happy to see him, and they spent the day catching up on all of his news.

Zia unlatched the hogan door knowing the sunrise awaited him. He thought, oh, how I've missed this—it feeds my soul. In Gallup there is no clear view of the sunrise—no open landscape to take it all in. Here the sun feeds the earth, and the mountains keep your spirits and your truths.

He recited the Daybreak Song, a Navajo legend of how the happy bluebird summons the sun to the sky every morning.

All night the gods were with us,
Now night is gone;
Silence the rattle,
Sing the daybreak song,
For in the dawn Bluebird calls,
With voice melodious, Bluebird calls,
And out from his blankets of tumbled gray,
The Sun comes, combing his hair for the day.

After a few cups of coffee and two slices of fried Spam on a piece of white bread slathered with Miracle Whip, Zia made his farewell and headed for Albuquerque.

Zia got to Dr. Ortiz's office early, so her assistant could photocopy the latest installment of his project where he was detailing the Navajo arts and crafts training and retailing concept. This was the most unique section of his project where he stressed combining Navajo tradition with theory and practice.

"Where would you get the funding to execute this plan?" the dean quizzed.

"I'm not sure yet," Zia answered. "I've given this a lot of thought. I suppose we could go the route of grants or funding from the tribe, but part of me sees an entrepreneurial approach. Maybe people in the business of Indian arts and crafts could invest in the concept in hopes that it could become self-sustaining. I think it would strengthen the business and it's an investment in the future of the arts and crafts, as well."

Zia leaned forward and folded his hands and looked into the distance.

"I often wonder about the genius that might be discovered in this kind of educational setting. What if we could produce the next great artisans? What if we gave someone the educational opportunity of a lifetime? The possibilities fascinate me."

"That's noble of you, Mr. Yazzie, but I think you're a dreamer," the dean said.

"Maybe so, sir. But my mother tells me sad stories of the boarding schools where they tried to strip the children of their tribal identities and traditions. Maybe all theory and no practice fails for our students. Over the past few months, I've had some experiences that have opened my mind to a new way of thinking. I'm confident that a concept based in Navajo tradition could work."

"I think he makes a good argument," Dr. Ortiz said.

"Ramona, you're treating this like it could really happen," the dean said.

"Well," she huffed. "I think it could."

"People, people, this is an independent study, not a sales pitch," the department chair stated. "If this presentation is living up to your expectations, then that's what we're here for. Whether it comes to fruition or not is insignificant."

Zia sat quietly. He wanted this concept to satisfy the necessary credits to get his degree, but he was serious about it. Sure, seeing it happen seemed like a huge challenge, but sitting in a conference room debating it would never make it come to life. Zia realized that the few months he had spent away from the sterile and protected educational environment had jump-started his independent thinking. Maybe he was more like Ben Monroe than he wanted to admit. Maybe he didn't want to be a teacher after all. Maybe he wanted to be the administrator.

"Mr. Yazzie," the dean said. "It appears that you are making the proper progress on your independent study—whether I agree with the concept or not. Your next installment is due in two weeks...just before spring break."

Zia walked to the Frontier, where the place overflowed with students as usual. He glanced around and caught sight of Selene at a table in the back corner writing in a spiral notebook. He breathed a sigh of relief.

"Ya'at'eeh', Gallup girl. Long time no look."

"Hi, Zia, I was working on an essay for English."

"What's it about?" he said as he pulled up a chair and sat down.

"Actually, I decided to write it on last year's abortion issue, Roe vs. Wade, but I'm having trouble with my thesis statement to get the whole thing started. There is a ton of information at the library, so I shouldn't have any problems. I was just doing the 'what if's' in my head. I read that both Michaelangelo and Adolf Hitler were illegitimate children. So what if either had been aborted—how would that have changed our world?"

"That's heavy stuff, Selene. Actually, that might be a good thesis statement—the what if."

"Yes, you're right. That would set it up in a way that defends and questions the abortion issue. Thanks, Zia. You are going to be a great teacher."

"Funny you should say that. I've decided I don't want to be a teacher."

"You?"

"Oh, I'm still serious about education. I just want to be in charge of how things are taught and how they are run."

"Well, well. So you want to be the *chief*."

"Bad, Selene. Very bad." He shook his head. "I don't know about you, but I'm hungry."

"Me, too. It's almost Easter, and during Lent the abuelita is fixing nothing but beans and *chicos* or *chaquehue* and other meatless dishes. I feel like a hamburger."

"Sounds delicious. I'll order us each a cheeseburger…uh, with green chile strips?"

"That's the magic potion—green chile," she smiled. "How did your presentation go today, Zia?"

"They challenged me, but I got through it. The dean doesn't seem to like any approach to education that's out of the ordinary, tried-and-true kind of thing."

"I guess that's why he's the dean." Selene hit her fist on the table as if it were a gavel.

Their green chile cheeseburgers and fries arrived and they both dove into their lunches.

"I'm going to be here another day. Do you want to go to a movie or out for a bite to eat later?" Zia gulped awaiting her answer.

"Oh, I wish I could, but I've got to finish this essay. As usual, I waited until the last day." Then with a glint in her eyes, she said, "Zia, I could do something tomorrow. If I hurry and finish this essay and hand it in early, I can skip class tomorrow."

"Well, I was thinking of driving up to Santa Fe for part of the day. Would you be interested?"

"That would be fun. When do you plan to leave?"

"Early. I'm all about sunrise."

"Oh, that's right *Zia*, Mr. Sunshine, and I'm all about moonlight."

"Can we compromise and leave about 9 tomorrow?"

"Sure. That way we can make it to the La Fonda in time for a late breakfast, so you wouldn't be without green chile for more than 24 hours."

Selene told Zia how to get to her abuelita's house just east of the campus.

"Whatever you do, don't tell her we're going to Santa Fe. She'll want to come along and have us drop her off at the archives."

Zia shrugged his shoulders and gave her a look of disbelief.

"I'm not kidding," Selene insisted.

Zia was curious to meet the abuelita, and she lived up to his expectations. A small slender woman with angular features and gray eyes like Selene's, she wore a blue plaid house dress and a hand-knitted black sweater. Long warm socks stretched up her thin legs with soft moccasins on her feet. Her white hair was pulled back in a tight bun and round glasses were planted on the bridge of her nose.

Selene had warned her not to mention the Navajos raiding her ancestors' village of Cebolleta.

"*Abuelita, te presento mi amigo*, Zia Yazzie."

"*Con mucho gusto*, Zia," she said as she held out a thin boney hand.

"It's nice to meet you," Zia replied giving her a gentle handshake.

"Well, it's a sunny day, so we thought we'd go for a ride and get a bite to eat," Zia said.

"It is another pretty day," the abuelita agreed. "The fruit trees are even starting to bud. That means we'll surely get another freeze and my nectarines will be ruined again this year. Ay Dios."

Selene motioned to Zia to start making their exit.

The drive took about an hour, and the final climb up La Bajada hill to the 7,000-foot elevation brought the adobe landscape of Santa Fe into view in the distance.

Selene sighed. "I love Santa Fe. There's something magical about it—the historical roots, the architecture, the culture. It's beautiful. Too bad Gallup doesn't look like this."

Zia chuckled and continued driving as close as he could to the Plaza and found a parking place. The air was brisk and cool, but the New Mexico sun shone bright and warming, and there wasn't a cloud in the high-desert blue sky.

After a quick walk, they rounded the corner to where the La Fonda Hotel stood at the edge of the historic Plaza—the end of the Santa Fe Trail.

Selene put her hands on her hips and gazed lovingly at the La Fonda. "You know, Zia, a woman architect designed this—Mary Colter. Look at how the adobe structure flows with those soft lines. It's a landmark."

"Look up there," she said pointing to the second story. "That's where JFK and Jackie stayed when they visited Santa Fe…in that room. I want to stay in that room someday and stroll out on the balcony that overlooks the Plaza and try to imagine what Jackie thought of it—maybe for Indian Market or Fiesta," she sighed.

"Well, you better book the room soon, aren't those two of the busiest times here?"

"Oh, well, dream on. Shall we go in, Zia?"

The dark stone floors of the lobby shone beautifully against the hand-carved fixtures, and the corner fireplace held the remains of an early-morning fire and the luscious scent of burned piñon logs. The bright and airy glass-enclosed restaurant with its window panes individually painted in colorful designs and traditional symbols was inviting. Rugged hand-hewn chairs and tables were set with starched white linens—blending the formal with the rustic.

They sipped on perfectly brewed coffee and glanced at the tall leather-bound menus.

"Mmm, everything looks so good, Zia. What are you going to have?"

"I'm thinking of huevos rancheros with red chile and posole on the side."

"Well that's a good choice. Maybe I should have the same thing and ask for a little bowl of green chile, too. Do you want to try their green chile?"

"Sure."

Selene looked like she belonged to Santa Fe. Her jeans, boots, concho belt and leather jacket made her appear to be a local. Zia thought the Spanish girls of northern New Mexico were the prettiest girls anywhere, and Selene definitely possessed those looks. He had dated a few Navajo girls from Thoreau, and a few at UNM, but Selene was the first Spanish girl that he was really interested in.

"Zia, what are you thinking?"

"Nothing really, I guess my mind was wandering."

"Zia, tell me more about yourself? Do you have any brothers and sisters—what about your parents?"

No way, he thought. My carefully built wall isn't going to crumble under her scrutiny. I really don't want her to know about Ben or any of that part of my life until it's resolved. Gossip goes through Gallup like a wild dust devil. I wouldn't want her to mention it to someone who knows my half-sister.

"Actually, I'm an only child, but I'm part of a large clan. My mother is a teacher's aide in the Head Start program in Thoreau at St. Bonaventure's."

"So, she made sure you had a good education?"

"Oh, yes. She never stopped encouraging me. She even let me read by flashlight late at night when it was dark in the hogan. Then she would drill me on my multiplication tables in the morning before school. When she was a girl, she was forced to go away to boarding school and was terribly lonely, but she was getting a good education. It all stopped when she was 16 and had me. I'm sure that's why it's so important to her that I succeed."

"What about your father?"

"He wasn't around, but he did the honorable thing by supporting my mother and me."

"Zia, this is a weird question. Do you feel different than other Navajos?"

He squirmed and took a sip of coffee. "Growing up, I felt completely Navajo. Now...well, now I feel that there's another part of me I have to discover. Does that make sense?"

"I guess. I suppose I can't really comprehend the influence of the opposite worlds you're connected to. Can you exist in both?"

"I have to."

"What about you, Moonbeam?"

"Well, by comparison, I'm just a spoiled Gallup kid, living off the profits of Indian jewelry."

"There's a lot of that happening in Gallup these days."

"How did you end up in Gallup, Zia?"

"That's a long story, Selene. I'll save it for another day. Let's take a walk around the Plaza and do some sightseeing.

They wandered around the Plaza, in and out of the many shops. Packard's fascinated Zia with its gorgeous Indian jewelry and pottery. Against one far wall, Navajo rugs hung individually from ceiling to floor as if they were in a giant open closet. Zia was amazed with their beauty and impressed with the skillful weaving—some were as large as 9 x 12 feet.

"Do you realize the work that went into these fantastic tapestries, Selene? I'm in awe."

"I'm in awe of the prices," she commented.

At the Palace of the Governor's, as usual, some Indian artisans had their blankets spread on the walkway of the portal with goods to sell, but since there weren't many tourists in the winter months, there weren't many vendors, either. The items sold there couldn't compare to what was found in the shops and galleries.

Meandering from shop to shop, Zia noticed all the window displays, examined how the showcases were fashioned and placed in the store and studied the jewelry displays. Since these merchants weren't in the business of wholesaling, their stores presented more of a gallery look—more unique and high-priced pieces, some even displayed ribbons won on specific pieces at Indian Market the past summer. This was the place for collectors.

"I'd like to come back here for Indian Market this summer. How about you, Selene?"

"Yes, I'd love it."

Zia wondered if maybe by then he would know her well enough to reserve the JFK and Jackie room.

Back to reality, Zia knew he needed to understand and experience another level of the business—for two reasons, Monroe's and his proposal for the Navajo Arts and Crafts Academy. Indian Market was a juried show, which meant only the best would be in attendance. He wondered how he could apply these artisan's skills to the Academy. Would any of them be interested in teaching? How did they achieve this level of expertise?

"Zia, there's so much more to see and do here, but I'm getting cold. I think the weather is changing."

"You're right. Let's come here again in the warmer months. I need to get back to Gallup later today anyway."

The drive back to Albuquerque took little more than an hour, and they both agreed it had been nice to escape for a while.

When Zia pulled up in front of the abuelita's house, Selene leaned over and kissed him on the cheek.

"Zia, I like you. You're not like the other guys I know."

"Half of me is."

***

Luz grabbed a handful of dry pinto beans from the large gunny sack and meticulously sorted them looking for small stones. Handful after handful, her skillful bean-cleaning was soon completed.

Ben and Cecelia sat at the kitchen table drinking coffee and reading the newspaper.

Ben seems anxious about something, Cecelia thought. It's just a feeling, I guess. It's probably because I'm so bored with my life that I'm inventing things. Selene is away at college and Luz does everything around here. I feel so useless.

"How are sales going with O'Malley's Gems & Jewels, Ben?"

"Actually, really well. They are beginning to re-order. We did a great job of choosing the basic selection. Everything is selling."

Oh, he thought, and by the way, I have a half-Navajo, 21-year-old son. So, when am I going to have the nerve to tell her?

"We're going to be busier than ever this summer, so I'm expecting Selene to work in the store. Do you want to prepare her, or should I?"

"You tell her, Ben."

"Okay, I'll call her tomorrow." Hmm, he thought, or maybe I'll just wait until spring break when she's home and tell her about her half-brother, too.

Luz mumbled, *"Mañana, mañana,"* while she chopped an onion to toss into the bean pot.

"What did you say, Luz?" Ben asked.

"Mañana. Mañana. There's an old saying, Señor Ben—'mañana is the busiest day of the week.'"

Boy, did that hit a nerve, he thought.

"Okay, Ben, I'll prepare Selene for the inevitability of working in the store this summer. I'll do it 'mañana,' of course," Cecelia laughed.

"You know I could work in the store, too," Cecelia stated.

Ben pretended he didn't hear her.

Cecelia sighed. I know he'll never ask me to help with anything at the store or any future ventures. To him, I'm just a housewife, and he is the ruler and provider. What a trap.

"Do you want Selene to start during spring break to get used to things?"

Hell no, Ben thought. That would be a disaster with Zia there. I've got to confess and get this over with soon. Mañana may be a deadly day for me!

"No, let her have her vacation. As soon as the semester is over, she'll have to be ready to start. It's payback time."

Luz added a dollop of lard to the boiling pot of beans before she positioned the lid, and lowered the gas to let them simmer for several hours. If I were Selene, she thought, I'd be signing up for summer school.

***

As soon as Ben parked his car in front of the store, Navajo and Zuni jewelers appeared with brown paper sacks filled with jewelry to sell—especially on Saturdays when huge numbers from the outlying reservations came to Gallup to shop, eat out and sell arts and crafts to the traders.

He motioned Mary Largo to the showcase at the back of the store. The Navajo silversmith did an expert job of oxidizing the silver in her ring and bracelet sets, and her work had clean lines. Her bezels were fine and smooth and held the combination of turquoise and coral stones symmetrically. She always signed her work—which the traders encouraged and the buyers appreciated. After they agreed on a price, Ben wrote the figures and total on the bag with his black marker and took Mary Largo and the bag of jewelry to Louise for payment.

Zia watched and jotted Mary Largo's name and what Ben paid in his notebook. He had to be sure of the prices if she came back when he was buying. He had greeted her in Navajo and she remembered that he was from Thoreau, because she lived east of there, close to Prewitt.

"Just stay here with me and study this process," Ben said as he signaled another Navajo woman to the showcase with her two small children in tow.

Jerry knew to watch the store and wait on customers. He had a knack for selling and a love for earning commissions.

Ben greeted them in Navajo and spread the jewelry out on a piece of black velvet to examine the workmanship and evaluate the price. The woman insisted on more than Ben offered. "That's not enough for my jewelries," she said. "I have to feed my sheeps, too, you know." Her face split into a smile. He upped his offer a bit, and they finally agreed. Before they left, Ben reached into his pocket and gave each of the children a dollar.

"This is for ice cream," he said.

They smiled shyly and thanked him.

Zia put his hands in his pockets and turned and smiled to himself. Those kids knew he was going to give each of them a dollar—he does it every time.

When the buying was finished, Ben lit up a Marlboro and told Zia he wanted him to go to Zuni with him the following day to get familiar with buying there.

"I have a few silversmiths I'd like you to meet. I can't be down there every day to buy, so I count on the Arabs. They're always in Zuni, and they do a good job."

The drive to Zuni took about 30 minutes and the landscape of rolling hills, piñon and juniper was prettier than the barren backdrop of Gallup. Ben smoked and talked business while Zia took in the scenery—and cracked the window and let in a little fresh air.

The quaint, historic pueblo of Zuni soon came into view. Squat stone houses surrounded the traditional plaza, each with an adobe *horno* outside for baking thick, crusty Pueblo bread.

"The Pueblos are so much different than the Navajos," Zia commented. "We're spread out over our vast reservation, and they live within a village."

"It is different, and it's such a pretty place. Just ahead, you'll see the old mission church, and then we'll stop at a few of the silversmiths' houses."

"I want to get some of Horace Iule's crosses, some channel-work inlay from the Quandelacy's, some inlaid owl jewelry from Lesansee. We need a few showy cluster pieces from Leonard and Edith Lonjose, and some Pete Haloo petit-point. And I like the work the Panteahs have been doing lately. It's colorful and original and more modern."

"Zia, don't let me forget, my housekeeper wants a few loaves of horno bread."

Ben wandered around the village to various dwellings and managed to find some beautiful work. Zia paid close attention.

"I'm getting a whole new appreciation for Zuni jewelry," Zia said.

"That's good. They do wonderful work."

Over lunch at Pat's Chile Parlor in Zuni, Ben talked about El

Morro—Inscription Rock, just down the highway toward the Ice Caves.

"It makes a good day trip. You should go there sometime. It's a great hike, and you can see where the conquistadors passed through in the late 1500s and early 1600s. They stopped at a natural spring to water their horses, then carved their names and the dates on the smooth rock above the pond. History, right before your eyes."

"That's a good idea, Ben. I have a friend from school who is coming home to Gallup for spring break. I think I'll take her there on my day off."

"Well, always glad to help out with your social life."

***

Spring break was quickly approaching, and Zia had his presentation handwritten and ready for Louise, and he was more anxious than ever to see Selene. It was time to make his move.

The trip to Zuni had sparked a new idea for Zia's Academy. What if, as part of the function of the institution, they could train and certify professionals who worked in the Indian arts and crafts business—clerks in retail stores, galleries, museums? Why not? Even members of the general public could become certified to satisfy their own interests. The Academy could develop a program and charge a fee for earning certification. That would provide another stream of income as well as more credibility.

This will probably push the dean over the edge this week, he thought.

Zia had spent the last few mornings before work at Boyd's refining the new section of his presentation and now he felt confident that his idea would actually work. He never discussed his concept with Ben—he would probably think it was a waste of time or merely a work of fiction.

Thursday came quickly, and Zia met the sunrise as he drove by Red Rock State Park and recited the Beauty Way prayer to ensure a successful day.

The meeting began on time, with Dr. Ortiz showing her usual enthusiasm, while the dean and department chair quietly perused today's section of the proposal.

"This is preposterous, Mr. Yazzie," the dean said looking over the top of his glasses. "You can't have the accreditation to certify people as professionals in Indian arts and crafts."

"I think *reputation* is more important in this concept than accreditation," Ramona Ortiz countered.

"Okay, in this proposal he writes: 'A socially responsible institution, The Navajo Arts and Crafts Academy can create a vital program which would not only instruct and educate students, but also enlighten and inform the community, contributing to the respect due the artistry of the native peoples.' That says it all for me," Ramona Ortiz stated.

"Your concept seems to be getting more entrepreneurial," the department chair said scratching his head.

"I guess you could say that, sir, because I see this as a valid stream of income for the Academy. And, I think if we produce good artisans then we can have art shows and contests, too. This would bring us a lot of support from the traders—maybe even some scholarship money."

"I still think it's preposterous," the dean repeated. "If this academy of yours ever comes to fruition, I'll be there to cut the ribbon on opening day."

Zia clenched his teeth to prevent a grin spreading across his face.

"Ribbon cutting is for White people…we'll have a Medicine Man there to bless the school."

The department chair interrupted. "From what I can see, you have presented another section that meets the requirements for your independent study, and we'll await your next installment."

"Yes, *show time*," the dean said.

Everyone got up and started out of the conference room. Dr. Ortiz followed Zia out the door. "The dean is such a stick-in-the-mud. Personally, I can't wait for the next section of your proposal. I think it's fascinating."

"Thanks, Dr. Ortiz. See you soon."

Zia strolled toward the Frontier, anxious to see Selene.

It was a perfect day—warm, no wind. As he looked up toward the snow-topped Sandia Peak, he got an idea.

When he saw Selene crossing the street to the restaurant, he jogged up beside her and caught her by the elbow.

"Ay Dios."

"You have a Navajo sneaking up on you."

"So, what are you going to do now that you've captured me?"

"I have a plan of attack," Zia grinned. "It starts with skipping lunch here and taking the tramway up to the top of Sandia Peak. I've never been there. We can have lunch up there and enjoy the views."

Selene stepped back.

"I've never been there, either…and, uh, I'm afraid of heights," she said.

"Well, I'm afraid of Spanish girls—but I am enjoying the view," he said, taking hold of Selene's hand and looking her up and down. "C'mon, it'll be a new adventure."

"Okay, I'll try it. I might have to hold onto you for dear life going two miles up the side of that mountain in that contraption."

"The prospects are getting better by the minute," Zia smiled. "Let's go. Oh, it might be cold at the top. It's over 10,000 feet. Do you have a jacket?"

"In my car—it's across the street. Do you want me to drive?"

"No, I'll drive. We can just grab your jacket on the way to the truck."

When she opened the car, Zia inhaled the familiar scent of sweet perfume—just like Karen's. Selene never wore perfume. "Strange."

"What?" she said.

"It's that perfume smell."

"It came with the car, and it reeks. I can't wait until it's a bit warmer, and I can keep the windows down and air it out."

This has to be Karen's car, Zia thought. How in the world did Selene end up with it?

The drive to the tramway took them to the outskirts of town.

Zia paid for their tickets, and when they got on the tram it was nearly half full of tourists. Selene appeared reluctant.

"Okay, I'll sit by the window, so you don't have to look directly out."

She slid in next to him—close enough that he put his arm around her.

"Are you ready? Soon we'll be on top of the world."

When they reached the top and stepped out onto the platform, the panoramic view of the Rio Grande Valley was breathtaking.

"I can see Santa Fe, Zia. And look, there's Jemez Pueblo and the red cliffs."

"That's Mount Taylor," Zia said, looking west. "It's one of the four sacred mountains of the Navajos—Turquoise Mountain, and it's the mother of thunderstorms. I love to go up there during the summer rainy season and wait to hear the thunder, and smell the rain…then watch for the mist that hides the forest."

"That's fascinating. Will you take me there sometime?"

"Sure."

He leaned over and kissed her—a long and tender kiss and held her close.

He stroked her dark hair, then put his hand under her chin and looked deep into her gray eyes. "I want to get to know you better, Selene," he whispered. Lots better."

"It's about time, Zia!"

Ah, life is really good after all, he thought.

***

Spring break arrived, and Selene was anxious to spend an entire Thursday with Zia. She drove to Boyd's where they were meeting for breakfast before heading to El Morro—thinking of the possibilities the day might bring. She felt comfortable with him and recalled what Luz had told her many times that karma, destiny and fate brings people together.

"Hi, Zia," she waved and smiled as she got out of her car. "I'll leave the picnic basket in here until we're ready to leave."

"Okay," he said as he strode over to meet her.

"Well, Selene, you're looking beautiful as ever."

"Thanks. I wore my best Levis, denim shirt—and hiking boots for the trek."

"We'll have to have a good breakfast so we have the strength for a hike. Who knows what's in store for lunch."

"Don't worry. Luz made it, so you can be sure it will be delicious."

"But you're in charge of dessert," she said with a wink.

"Hmm, and I know exactly what I want."

After breakfast, they drove south of Gallup where the hilly landscape of juniper and piñon stretched out in front of them. At the Zuni junction, they headed east where the scenery held a backdrop of sandstone bluffs.

"Zia, what do you think will happen when you graduate? Will you stay in Gallup or come back to Albuquerque?"

"I don't know. I've been agonizing over it. I have a commitment in Gallup, but I have to get on with my life, too. Then there's money. I backed myself into a corner not wanting to teach anymore, and my 'lofty idea,' as the dean put it, needs some serious financing. So, I guess I'm stuck in Gallup for a while, Selene. You'll be here for the summer, won't you?"

"Oh yes, but knowing you'll be in town will make all the difference."

Zia reached over and placed his hand on her thigh and she covered his hand with hers. "I can't wait."

Finally, she thought, I found Zia—someone I can trust to have a genuine relationship.

"Look, there's El Morro—that sandstone mountain just ahead. I haven't been here for years. Zia, we'll have to take the trail to the top and see the Indian ruins. It's a nice hike, and you get a fantastic view from up there."

Suddenly, Zia slammed on the brakes to avoid hitting a coyote that darted across the road in front of the truck. He smacked the steering wheel with his hand and whispered something in Navajo.

"A coyote crossing your path means bad luck to a Navajo. If my mother was in this pickup, we would have to turn around and go back. But I'm not as superstitious."

"I never knew that."

"It's a Navajo signal that something bad is going to happen. The coyote is the messenger."

Please, he thought. Not today. Nothing bad is going to happen today.

Soon they pulled into the parking lot. They were surprised to see so many cars at the remote national monument. Inside the visitor's center, Zia paid their fee and received two guide books, and they headed up the half-mile trail to Inscription Rock.

"There it is, Zia. The pool of water sits against that sheer sandstone bluff. The conquistadors stopped here at the watering hole and carved their names into the soft stone."

"This one is my favorite, Zia," she said pointing to the ornate carving. "It begins, '*Pasó por Aqui, Juan de Oñate*'…and goes on, and translates to, 'Passed by here the Governor Don Juan de Oñate from the discovery the Sea of the South on 16th of April, 1605.' The abuelita says that meant the Gulf of California, but she doesn't believe he ever got there. "

"Fascinating—I'm glad we came here, Selene."

They followed the narrow, winding trail upward where spectacular views welcomed them at the crest—the Zuni Mountains in the distance and the volcanic craters of El Malpaís. They explored the ancient Pueblo ruins abandoned over 700 years earlier.

"The other day in Zuni, I was talking about the difference in the Pueblo people living in a community and the Navajos spread out over a huge reservation. We only take the land we need, though—nothing more."

"I'm glad that works for Navajos, Zia."

"In the Navajo Way, we are taught to value people above things—not compete for possessions."

"That's very honorable," she said, spreading her arms out and turning a full circle.

"Okay, Zia, I've had enough sightseeing. I'm ready for our picnic. Where to?"

"We'll just climb off this mountaintop and drive into the wilderness."

When Zia drove out of the monument's entrance, he headed east then suddenly turned off the highway and bumped along the countryside, leaving a trail of dust in their pathway.

"Is this how Navajos go on picnics?"

"I don't know, I've never been on a picnic. What do you have in that basket, anyway?"

"Fried chicken, potato chips, some small cans of juice and a few homemade chocolate chip cookies."

"Mmm, what's that saying White people use? 'The quickest way to a man's heart is through his stomach.'"

"That hurts. I thought you already liked me better than a chicken leg?"

"You're right. Forget lunch."

Zia stopped the truck and let the dust settle before they got out. Then he grabbed a blanket from behind the seat.

"You brought a blanket?"

"I'm Navajo, remember. I always carry a blanket. I have a canteen, some fire wood and matches back there, too. We could get stuck out here all night," he grinned.

They enjoyed their picnic lunch, and when Zia finished the last of his cookie, Selene moved up next to him. "Let me get that cookie crumb off your lip," as she leaned over to kiss him.

He grabbed her close and pulled her down on the blanket and they kissed and embraced like they couldn't get enough of one another.

"Hey, what do you kids think you're doing?"

Startled, the two jumped up to see a crusty old rancher on horseback resting a rifle across his lap. Selene buttoned and straightened her shirt and Zia stood up quickly.

"We're sorry, sir. We didn't know."

"What, didn't know whose land this is? Kids are always coming around here trying to screw around and mess up my property. You drive over my land and put ruts everywhere and smash the good grasses. I have cattle to feed. Now get the hell out of here," he commanded lifting the rifle and motioning toward the highway.

Selene grabbed the picnic basket and Zia bundled the blanket up and they threw everything in the back of the pickup and hopped in and drove out on the same ruts they had made coming in.

"This just isn't my day," Zia groaned. Maybe that coyote was giving me a signal after all, he thought.

"It was really nice until John Wayne showed up and ruined everything, Zia. I guess we should just go home."

"Well, maybe you could come over to my apartment?"

"Okay. First could we drop the picnic basket off at my house, and I'll tell my mom we're going to go do something."

"Do something? Are you blushing, Selene?"

They drove back to Gallup, and Selene directed him to her

home.

"This is the house. Just park in front, everyone parks in the back and there's no space left."

"I'll get the picnic basket for you. It will be nice to see your mom again. I want her to get used to having me around."

A bright grin slid across Selene's face.

When they strolled through the front door, Zia noticed the fine Navajo rugs spread on the stone floor and the array of pottery on the mantle—the best.

"Wow, Selene, who's the collector?"

"Oh, my dad. That's his life."

"Beautiful!"

"Let's go to the kitchen. That's where Mom and Luz will be."

The two women sat at the big wooden table drinking coffee. Cecelia got up when she saw them and hugged her daughter and shook Zia's hand.

"Nice to see you again, Zia. How was El Morro?"

"Really interesting. And, the picnic lunch was fantastic. Thank you," he said, putting the basket on the table.

"Luz is the best cook around," Cecelia said.

"I don't think you've officially met," she said introducing Zia to Luz.

He gave her a hearty handshake. "Well, I've officially eaten the best fried chicken ever. Great to meet you Luz, Selene brags about you all the time."

"Can you stay for coffee? Luz made some biscochitos, too."

"Sure, Mom. Then we're going out to finish the day's adventures."

They sat around the table and discussed El Morro. Then Ben strolled in through the back door and froze—staring at Zia, his face turned red and his lips whitened with anger.

"What are *you* doing here?"

Zia jumped up in shock to see Ben standing in front of him. He was speechless.

Selene turned ashen.

"This is my house—my family—my daughter."

"What do you mean?" Zia's voice quaked as he turned to Selene. "You never told me Ben Monroe was your father, Selene."

Zia's insides roiled. He could barely breathe.

"Why? What difference does it make?"

"Ask him!" he thundered, anger locked in his voice, pointing to Ben.

Zia scalded Ben with a look, then turned and ran out the front door. His breath came in gasps. His hands shook as he started the truck. His knees quivered as he tried to drive. Where should he go? The dark cloud of taboo hovered over him. He knew he was cursed for falling in love with his own sister.

I need a Medicine Man, he thought. I must be purged of this taboo. But I'll never get rid of the humiliation and heartbreak.

A seething hatred toward Ben Monroe raged in his gut. His life was ruined.

I've never felt such anger, he thought. It feels like I could explode. I will never face Ben Monroe again—and I can't set eyes on Selene ever again either. How could Ben have let this secret about me fester like this? If I had known Selene was my sister, I would never have allowed myself to be attracted to her.

Zia drove to the apartment, knowing he had to leave—run and heal himself…become Navajo again. He gathered his clothes and books and shoved what he could in his knapsack and put the rest in a grocery sack. He dropped the keys to the apartment, the truck and the store on the kitchen counter and walked to the train depot.

The schedule showed that the Amtrac to Albuquerque left in two hours. He bought a ticket and sat on the bench in a whirl of emotion and disgust—with a dark existence ahead of him. His roommates would probably be gone for spring break, so he could wallow in his misery while he developed a plan. He couldn't let his mother know. She would be too hurt.

I'll hop on that train and become invisible.

***

Luz moved away from the scene where Cecelia and Selene stood silent and bewildered, staring at Ben. It's so quiet in here, you could hear a mouse pee on a cotton ball, Luz thought.

"What just happened here, Ben?" Cecelia demanded.

"It's a long story." He looked like a wildcat caught in a trap.

"What did Zia ever do to you to make you so mean to him, Dad?" Selene yelled as tears sprang from her eyes. "How could you do this to me? I've never been so humiliated in my life."

"Calm down everyone," Luz commanded. "You're growing donkey ears here. Now just let Señor Ben explain."

Ben lit a cigarette, paced and ran his fingers through his hair. His anger seemed to soften as if his mind had wandered far away. Then he took a deep breath and turned toward the three women's stares.

"Zia is my son."

Cecelia gasped.

Luz shook her head and turned away. "Things will never be the same again," she whispered.

Selene screamed, then sobbed and ran toward the stairs.

"Let me finish the story, Selene."

She turned to him and gasped. "I know the story, Dad, I just never expected Zia's father to be *you*! I hate you for that, Dad. You've ruined my life. " She ran up the stairs sobbing and slammed the door to her room.

Ben shoved his hands in his pockets, put his head down and paced, thinking. What the hell is happening? I thought I could control the announcement and the outcome of the news and then everyone would accept Zia and it would be over. Now this! My son and my daughter are what—in love with each other? Impossible.

He walked to the kitchen counter and grabbed his keys.

"I'm leaving. I have to find Zia and talk to him—see if I can calm him down."

God dammit, why did I ever bring him around here in the first place, he wondered.

"We need to talk, Ben," Cecelia pleaded.

"Not now, dammit." His jaw was set in anger and his lips were white with fury.

Ben stomped out. The door slammed behind him. I'll suffocate if I stay there with them one more minute, he thought.

"Oh, Luz, what are we going to do? Poor Selene," tears welled up in Cecelia's eyes.

"*Siéntete*, CeCe, I'll pour us some coffee. *Cálmate.*"

Luz walked toward the coffee pot, pondering her response. Ay Dios, what I can possibly tell CeCe to make her feel better. What about her own secret? Is it time to confess? Or would that take the guilt away from Ben and put it on CeCe? Hmm, then poor Selene would be betrayed twice.

"*La verdad duela*, CeCe—the truth hurts."

"Now what do I do, Luz, just sit here and wait for the next shoe to drop?"

"I'd say that next shoe is on *your* foot, CeCe. You know, there's no *statue* of limitations on the truth."

"It's statute, Luz, and I'm not ready for that truth tonight, dammit!"

"Well, you better get ready. You have a daughter upstairs with a broken heart and a Navajo boy who thinks he has done something evil with his own sister who isn't even his sister. They are the victims of *two* lies."

I knew there was something familiar about that boy the first time I saw him, Luz thought. It must be my sick sense that picked up on it. He looks like a Navajo Ben Monroe.

"There's no escaping the truth, CeCe. That lie owns you. It took over your life and swallowed up your spirit."

Tears streamed down Cecelia's cheeks, drops falling onto the table as she sat holding the coffee mug and staring.

After several minutes, Cecelia came out of her trance and spoke in a whisper.

"Luz, I finally understand. When I told Ben I was pregnant, I expected to break up with him because it was David's baby. I was terrified. I figured I would go back and live with the abuelita, have the baby and struggle to raise it. Ben didn't even give me a chance to explain. He whisked me off to Las Vegas to get married, assuming it was his child. Of course, you know that, but here's what I realize now. He did that because he already had one illegitimate child and wouldn't let that happen again. It was responsibility, Luz, not love that motivated him."

"You're right. And you were so young and afraid. You knew he would be successful and could provide for you. CeCe, your lie locked up your heart, and you never let yourself love him, either."

A new rush of tears spilled from Cecelia's eyes.

"But why didn't he tell me about Zia, Luz?"

"*No sé*. Only he knows that.

"What are you going to do, CeCe?"

"I better quit thinking about myself and go console my daughter."

Cecelia walked out of the kitchen and through the living room and turned to climb the stairs. When she reached the landing, she noticed Selene's door ajar—she was gone.

***

Tears stung at Selene's eyes as she ran down the street—a sick feeling locked in the pit of her stomach.

Where do I go? What do I do now, she wondered? This is the worst day of my life. Finally, I found someone that I trusted. I think I was falling in love with him. Now this—he's my brother! I can't face anyone.

She kept running until she got to her car, parked across the street from Boyd's. Then she drove up and down the hilly streets of Gallup—over and over again—in a daze. She drove the length of Route 66 and back again, past the train depot where Zia sat waiting for the train to Albuquerque.

Stopped at the light, she watched two guys slip out of a dive that locals called the "queer bar." A double take told her one of them was Jerry.

"That does it! Oh God, I've had enough. I'm going back to Albuquerque where I can hide."

When she pulled up behind the house, she saw immediately that both her mother's and father's cars were gone. Good. She didn't want to face either of them.

She slipped in the back door and saw Luz sitting at the kitchen table—just sitting there staring. Luz jumped up when she saw her. "Ay Dios."

Selene marched into the kitchen.

"I'm packing up and going back to Albuquerque. I can't stay here." Tears streamed down her face. She was trembling.

"I understand," Luz said as she got up and rushed to put her arms around Selene and held her close. Selene sobbed.

"I can't imagine how hurt you must feel. But things will change, you'll see. The worst part of a problem is the beginning."

***

Zia sat next to the train window that faced north and watched the darkening landscape rumble by. As the red sandstone cliffs of Thoreau appeared, he sank into his seat in disgust, knowing he couldn't face his mother yet.

I'm nothing more than a half-breed bastard, he thought.

If Ben Monroe had been fair and honest, he thought, he and his sister would have known one another since they were children, and this would never have happened.

Zia understood the matriarchal society of the Navajo, where children belong to the mother's clan and are "born for" the father's clan. So in his traditional upbringing, he knew that to date or marry someone that closely related was considered incest, and Navajo spiritual practice was necessary. He would need the Medicine Man's ceremony to restore him to *Hozhó*—beauty, harmony, balance and health—though he didn't feel anything could restore him.

***

Ben found the apartment empty. Truck keys, store keys and apartment keys were thrown on the coffee table. Zia was gone. Now what?

Ben Monroe came home disgusted. He trudged through the back door of the house and saw Luz sitting at the kitchen table.

"Where is everyone?"

"Selene left for Albuquerque, and I don't know where CeCe went."

"So, why are you still here, Luz?"

You forget, she thought, I don't know how to drive, and I don't have a car.

"Ben, everything will work out. You'll see."

"Not this time, Luz. Not this time."

"I've been sitting here thinking for a while. I always say the worst part of a problem is the beginning, and I realized that everyone here needs to quit thinking about themselves—start thinking about each other."

"Everybody hates me. That's what I'm thinking."

Sure, he thought. While everybody is so busy thinking about themselves, I have a business to run—without Zia. I'm just furious as hell, that's what I am. Furious.

Cecelia stepped through the back door—her eyes red and puffy. She looked from Luz to Ben, then marched upstairs and slammed the bedroom door behind her and locked it.

She had a fifth of Scotch in her purse, and she intended to drink it all.

"Well, I guess I'm sleeping on the couch—so much for thinking about each other, Luz."

"La verdad duele, Señor Ben. The truth hurts."

Luz fingered the rosary in her apron pocket, thinking. And that goes for CeCe, too. It's her turn to deal with the truth, and it's more important now than ever.

Upstairs, Cecelia sat in bed and drank Scotch and cried. The more she drank, the more she cried. The more she cried, the more she drank.

I've lived with this lie so long, I can't part with it, she thought. More than that I don't want to be stripped of my deceit and have to reveal the person I have misrepresented all these years. I have never led an authentic life. What am I going to do? I've never told anyone, except Luz—but, of course, she was the one to figure it out. She'd been with our family since I was a little girl. She knows me better than my own mother.

Well, there's no getting out of it, Cecelia, she told herself. I'd better make a plan and... *come mierda*—eat shit! She downed the last of the Scotch and passed out.

***

When the abuelita walked into the kitchen to heat the kettle for her morning tea, Selene was sitting at the table.

"What are you doing here, Selena? I thought you weren't coming back until Sunday or Monday?" she said, surprised.

"I got back last night after you were asleep," she said, staring into oblivion.

"*¿Porqué?* You look dreadful."

Tears streamed from Selene's eyes hitting the old Formica table like raindrops, and low sobs began to ebb in her chest.

This is the same scene I witnessed nearly 20 years ago, the abuelita thought, when Cecelia found out she was pregnant. Maybe Selena is pregnant.

The old woman padded over to Selene, and swooped her up out of the chair and held her tightly, while her great-granddaughter cried her heart out.

"Whatever it is, mijita, I'll help you any way I can. Are you pregnant?"

"No, abuelita! Why do you think that?"

Selene dropped back into her chair. The abuelita sat down slowly across from her and wrapped her bony hands around Selene's.

"Because you reminded me so much of your mother when she found out she was pregnant with you. I'll never forget that day. I had already put the mal ojo on that *gavacho*, that David Stanfield. I never trusted him. I told Cecelia to go home and tell her parents. We would figure everything out. The next thing I knew, she ran off to Las Vegas to marry Ben Monroe."

"What are you talking about, abuelita?" Selene gasped, pulling her hands away. "My mother never told me any of this! That's not how it was. Mom said she started dating Dad when she worked at the El Rancho during the summer and that they would see each other whenever she was in Gallup. She said she got pregnant on their honeymoon."

Oh no, the abuelita thought, I should have kept quiet. *En boca cerrada, no entran moscas*—a closed mouth catches no flies.

Selene sat staring out the window. "You know something, abuelita? Remember when Mom and I went to meet Zia for lunch a while back when she brought my new car here. Well, we met David Stanfield and Mom told us she dated him while she was going to UNM. That's all."

The abuelita just shrugged her shoulders.

"Abuelita, did my mom tell you David Stanfield was my father?"

The abuelita was silent. She got up and walked toward the stove, then turned and sat down at the table again.

"I'm an old lady, what do I know?"

"She had been dating my dad. Maybe she lied to me about being pregnant before they got married to protect me. You know how old fashioned she is."

Sure, the abuelita thought, as she turned and rolled her eyes, so old fashioned that she was dating two guys at the same time—*sin verguenza*, shameless.

"Well, so much for that, mijita. That's ancient history. Tell me what happened to *you?*"

Tears clutched at Selene's eyes again, and she took a deep breath.

"You've met Zia, abuelita. We became friends, and we were starting to date. I really liked him. He's not like the other guys around here. Anyway, when I went home for spring break, we planned an outing to El Morro and a picnic. When we came home, I brought him in the house to say hi to Mom and introduce him to Luz before we went out again. Just then, Dad came through the door and went into a rampage."

"About what, mijita?"

"He was screaming at Zia about being there with his wife and daughter. Zia seemed like he was in shock—and infuriated. When I asked what was going on, Zia pointed at Dad and said to ask him, then Zia stormed out of the house."

"I don't understand, mijita."

"Abuelita, Zia is my father's illegitimate son. He had kept that a secret from everyone. He's my brother, abuelita…I was falling in love with my own brother."

Selene was sobbing again.

"I can never forgive my father for this. Never."

"I'm shocked, too. What did your mother tell you?"

"Nothing! I ran upstairs. When I left to walk down to where my car was parked, she was in the kitchen whispering with Luz. When I came home she was gone, and I told Luz I was going back to Albuquerque."

"What did Luz say?"

"That the worst part of a problem is the beginning. Yeah, the beginning of what? It feels more like the end to me."

The abuelita pushed herself up from her chair and headed to the stove and fired up the tea kettle, and Selene put her head in her hands and wept.

The abuelita turned with a start. "I don't get it, Selena. Didn't Zia know your last name is Monroe?"

"I didn't tell him…because I thought he would think I was the spoiled daughter of the town's rich Indian trader and not bother with me."

"Ay Dios, mijita. Ay Dios."

PART 4: THE NAVAJO WAY

Ben Monroe left the house at dawn—rumpled and unshaven. He believed Zia would be at his mother's hogan, and headed for Thoreau.

Anjelah was surprised to see him. "What's wrong, Ben? You look terrible. Did something happen to Zia?"

"He's not here, Angie?"

"No."

"What's wrong?" Terror and fear swept over her face.

"He hasn't been in an accident or anything, Angie. Don't worry. Can I come in and talk to you?"

"Of course. I'll make coffee."

Ben told Anjelah everything—probably the most in-depth conversation they'd had in years.

"My son needs a Medicine Man, a *hataalii*, right away. Where do you think Zia went, Ben?"

"I thought he would be here, but he probably went to Albuquerque. Can you give me his address and phone number there?"

"Of course."

"Bring him home to me, please," she whimpered, wringing her hands.

"I will. I promise."

She handed him a slip of paper with all the information. "This is the phone number at St. Bonaventure. You can call me there with any news."

***

Cecelia's head pounded from the bottle of Scotch she had drunk the night before. She downed two aspirins and dumped extra eye drops into her swollen, red eyes. She put on jeans, a sweatshirt and tennis shoes, and then pulled her hair back in a ponytail. Then she threw a few things in a bag, just in case she spent the night at the abuelita's house. One look in the mirror told her that she definitely needed sunglasses.

Downstairs, she had a cup of coffee with Luz and a piece of dry toast. Nothing seemed to help her.

"Luz, I'm going to Albuquerque to look for Selene."

"What are you going to tell her, CeCe?"

Cecelia wiped new tears from her eyes.

"I have the next two hours to figure that out."

Luz fingered the rosary in the pocket of her apron, praying for a miracle.

"Do you want me to go with you?"

"No, I have to face my demons on my own this time, Luz."

Cecelia trudged toward the kitchen door to leave.

"Just tell the truth, CeCe. You can't own tomorrow."

***

Ben headed back to Gallup and went directly to the store. He called the apartment in Albuquerque. No answer. Again and again. No answer. He called Louise at home.

"Louise…sorry to call so early. Do you think Fred can help out for the next several days? Zia won't be here…I'll explain later. I have to go to Albuquerque today, so I won't be around, either…okay. Thanks. I know you can handle everything."

Next, he cringed and called home.

"Hi, Luz, what's going on there? Have you heard from Selene? Is Cecelia there?"

Luz said there had been no word from Selene and that Cecelia had just left for Albuquerque.

Relieved that he didn't have to confront Cecelia, Ben went home, showered and packed a bag. He had to find Zia and face him—take him to his mother. Then he had to deal with Selene and Cecelia—get all this bullshit over with and get back to work.

***

The abuelita brewed tea and toasted two slices of homemade bread and spread it with her elderberry jam and tried to console Selene. She fumbled with her tea cup, trying to think of a way for Selena to find that box of her mother's things in the attic. Cecelia used to keep a diary.

"Selena, I'm working on my genealogy today, and I need a metal box from the attic that is full of old family papers. Can you go up and find it for me? I'm too old to climb that ladder and hunt around."

"Sure, abuelita. I'll do it right now."

Selene got a stool and opened the trap door and slid the ladder down. She climbed into the attic and let her eyes adjust, then found the string for the lone ceiling light.

The abuelita called up to her. "Okay Selena, it's a small olive green metal box—used to hold ammunition for the military—that snaps shut with hinges and has a handle."

"I'll get looking. There's a lot of stuff up here."

She rummaged around, moving things forward and back. Just as she located the green canister, she saw a box marked Cecelia—UNM.

Selene called down to the abuelita. "I found the green box for you. There's a box of my mom's things from college. Is it okay if I

153

look through them?"

"Sure, she has nothing to hide. Take your time."

The abuelita crossed herself and looked upward. Nothing to hide, she thought. I sure hope that child uncovers the truth up there.

"Looks like she saved all her books and got good grades," Selene shouted.

Then she found the diary, and silence set in.

Cecelia wrote about her dreams of working with foster children—becoming a social worker.

Selene looked up from the diary, wondering. I never knew my mother had dreams—unfulfilled dreams. Oh, here's the part about meeting my dad.

It read: "He's so handsome and such a flirt. He said our eyes met like magnets. Did I feel it, too?"

Oh yuck, she thought. That's awful.

She turned the page to read: "David Stanfield doesn't know about Ben—and Ben doesn't know about David, either. David is such an arrogant jerk. I know he's using me. I want it to be over. Ben is different—independent, exciting, adventurous. He has big plans for himself. He doesn't throw that intellectual superiority in my face like David does. Actually, he thinks college is a pure waste of time and money. The abuelita better never hear that."

The next few pages were wavy and rumpled and stuck together—must have gotten wet, Selene thought. She managed to carefully pry them apart, but some of the ink had run.

She trembled as she read: "I'm pregnant with David's baby. He'll just laugh at me and say I'm stupid when I tell him. Maybe I won't tell him—just have the baby and make the best of it. I'll just disappear out of his life. He couldn't care less. I'm afraid I have to tell Ben. I can't just disappear out of his life. He'll come looking for me."

That was the last entry. Selene guessed it was her mother's tears that had spilled onto the pages—like the ones falling from her own eyes now.

Selene grabbed the dark green container and the diary and climbed down from the attic. One look at her ashen, tear-stained face, and the abuelita knew.

***

Ben stopped for gas and called Zia's apartment from the station's phone booth. Just as he was about to hang up, a groggy voice said a raspy "Hello."

"I'm looking for Zia Yazzie."

"He left for Crownpoint to see a Medicine Man or something. He said he would be back in a few days."

"Did he say anything else?"

"Nope. I just got back from spring break. That's all he told me."

"Will you please ask him to call Ben Monroe? He knows the number."

"Okay."

Now, I better call Angie at St. Bonaventure's, Ben thought, and tell her Zia is on his way to Crownpoint to see a Medicine Man.

Ben stopped for a quick bite to eat and slugged down some

coffee. Next, he planned to show up at the abuelita's house for the final confrontation and accept the consequences of their disgust with him. But he would apologize for the pain he had caused.

***

"Abuelita! It's true. I'm as illegitimate as Zia. Look at this diary!" she sobbed, throwing it on the kitchen table and setting the metal box down next to it.

'Siéntete, mijita. Sit down here and we'll look at this together."

"It's all there, just like you said. David Stanfield is my real father—not Ben Monroe. My mother is a fraud and a liar." She wept.

"Cálmate. I'm sorry, mijita, this is shocking for you to learn. I don't know what to say," as her voice cracked, and her bony hands trembled now that Selene finally knew the truth.

A rap at the front door silenced them.

"Who could that be? Nobody ever comes here without calling first," the abuelita said.

She held onto the table and pushed herself up out of the chair and moved toward the door. Selene stared out the window toward Sandia Peak, tears filled her eyes.

"I have to see Selene," Cecelia cried as door opened.

The abuelita motioned toward the kitchen table, then crossed herself and said a silent prayer to St. Jude, the patron saint of hopeless causes.

Selene turned and looked at her mother with disgust—was silent, then turned away.

"Selene, I have to talk to you."

"You're twenty years too late, Mom," she screamed. "It's all here in your diary. I found it in the attic. I hate you for what you've done to me."

"Let me explain."

"Explain! You're a liar and a fraud."

Another knock at the door startled everyone into silence.

The abuelita shuffled to the door again, and there stood Ben Monroe.

"What's with all the screaming, abuelita?" Ben Monroe stepped in looking bewildered.

I figured they'd be better adjusted to the news by now, he thought.

He looked from Cecelia to Selene. They stood there silently, staring at him.

"I'm sorry," he said shrugging. "You can hate me for what I've done, but we have to get on with our lives. I especially regret what I've done to you, Selene—my own daughter."

She burst into tears. Cecelia sobbed.

Ay Dios, it's too late for St. Jude. It looks like I have to take over here—the last thing I wanted to do, the abuelita thought. She clapped her hands like a Mother Superior and silenced everyone.

"Ben, there's more to this story. You and Cecelia go into the living room," she commanded, directing them with a pointed finger. "This is between a husband and a wife."

"You, Selena, march into the bathroom and take a long shower and run a lot of hot water over your head, and change your attitude. The world doesn't revolve around you. Ay Dios, deal with it! '*Nada es fácil, pero todo es posible.* Nothing is easy, but anything is possible.'"

***

Zia boarded the bus for Crownpoint—north of Thoreau. It would take several hours to get there because the Continental Trailways stopped in every town along the way, and the last stop before Crownpoint was Thoreau. Zia didn't want to call attention to himself and his taboo by looking for the Medicine Man, the hitaalii, in Thoreau. To make matters worse, he didn't want his mother to know the evil he had encountered.

He knew of Hosteen Begay in Crownpoint, a well-known Medicine Man and gifted hand trembler. His ability made him able to see the problem and analyze the type of ceremony needed for healing the person.

As a young Navajo boy, Zia learned that medicine men who are hand tremblers receive their gift from the Gila Monster—that venomous lizard of the Southwest. The spirit of the Gila Monster makes the Medicine Man capable of going into a trancelike state where he passes his trembling hand over the individual and analyzes the cause of his problem and decides on the ceremonial solution.

I'm sure he'll want me in the sweat lodge, too, Zia thought. I need to repair the damage to my spirit, mind and body. There, maybe, just maybe, I can get some answers and guidance from the

Creator.

His ceremony would probably take several days because of the taboos violated upon him, he thought. Hosteen Begay would know whether he needed a Night Chant or a Dawn Ceremony.

The bus rumbled along, and his thoughts darted in many directions. So much revulsion. So much guilt. It played out in his mind like a broken record—over and over again. Finally, he slipped into sleep and dreamed of the first Enemy Way ceremony that was performed for Changing Woman's twin sons Monster Slayer and Born-for-the-Water after they had slain the Yéi giants and restored Hozhó to his people.

He awoke knowing he desperately needed Hozhó, the beauty, harmony and health that could possibly restore him from who he was now—a half-breed bastard in love with his sister.

***

"Okay, abuelita. Here I am all cleaned up…with a better attitude. Well, a little better, maybe."

The abuelita sat at the kitchen table with her cup of tea studying her family tree and glanced at Selene over her glasses.

"Selena, go into the living room!"

Jeez, Selene thought, she's like a damn judge and jury, and I'm the next one to take the stand.

Selene took a deep breath and walked in to face Ben and Cecelia—not knowing what to expect. Anger. Tears. Hatred.

Ben stood up.

"Selene, your mother and I have decided to try and work through some really difficult things here, and we need your cooperation and acceptance."

"I'll try," her voice quivered. "Where do we begin?"

"To begin with…as far as I'm concerned you *are* my daughter. Do you understand?"

"Yes…D…Dad." Tears filled her eyes. "I was so afraid of losing you. I was so angry that you weren't my dad and would reject me."

"Mom, I still can't understand why you did this to me and to Dad."

"I was young. I was afraid," she stuttered. "Afraid for myself, and afraid for you. The lie just grew into a monster. I feel like I've been released from a life sentence."

"Me, too," Ben said. I've kept Zia a secret for far too long."

"But Dad…what about Zia? What will happen to him?"

"I called his apartment this morning, and his roommate said he was on his way to Crownpoint to see a Medicine Man. According to his Navajo ways, he has to have the taboo lifted and his spirit healed. That takes a Medicine Man and a sing…could last for days."

"But he doesn't need that now. He's not my brother! Can't you get in touch with him?"

"Selene, I stopped and saw his mother this morning. I thought he'd be there. When I told her what happened, she was heartbroken and wants her son healed and brought back to her. I promised. I have to leave in a few minutes and drive to Crownpoint and find Zia."

"I'm going with you."

Ben shook his head no.

"I'm going with you, Dad. I owe it to Zia to tell him the truth myself."

"Alright then, dammit. Get your things together. We're leaving now."

***

Ben drove fast, smoking one cigarette after another and listening to an 8-track tape of Slim Whitman. It was obvious he wasn't in the mood to talk.

Selene stared out the car window and watched the familiar landscape speed by, thinking about how the abuelita had commanded her to "deal with it." The old woman is wise—and forceful—I'll give her that. I suppose I'd still be whining and screaming if she hadn't cut me off. Well, I still have the next hour or so to dwell on it—and that's exactly what I'm going to do.

Selene took a deep breath and stared trance-like into the vast landscape.

At the Thoreau exit, Selene pointed to Red Cliffs Trading Post. "There's Grandma and Grandpa's...do we have to explain all of this to them?"

"No, they're old-fashioned Bible thumpers. They nearly condemned me to hell when I told them I had gotten Angie pregnant. This would put them into a Baptist frenzy."

"Yes, I suppose we should protect them. We hardly ever see them anyway. Why is that?"

"I guess it's because I just work all the time. That's why I blame myself for never getting around to telling you and your mom about Zia. I was so busy trying to make more money."

"Because you're a workaholic?"

"I love what I do. Does that make me a workaholic?"

"I never thought of it that way before, Dad."

Ben turned up the red clay road to Anjelah's hogan.

"Where are we going?"

"I have to talk to Zia's mother and tell her about you. That will lift the taboo from Zia."

He parked next to the old blue pickup, and Selene stared in amazement at the hogan where Zia had grown up. She was anxious to meet Anjelah Yazzie, Zia's mother, and hopped out of the car.

"No! Get back in the car. You can't go in. To Angie, you are a living, breathing taboo and walking into her hogan would bring evil into her home. You have to stay here and let me explain everything to her. You have to understand the ways of the Navajo."

"Okay."

After what seemed a long time, Ben returned to the car.

"Angie thinks Zia is on his way to see Hosteen Begay. He's a well-respected Medicine Man and a hand trembler."

"What's a hand trembler?"

"He has special powers and insights—like a seer."

"Why is he called Hosteen, Dad?"

"Hosteen is a term of honor and respect."

Selene nodded her head. "Okay, I understand."

"Enough questions. Now, this is the plan, Selene. Angie will drive ahead of us, because she knows where to find the Medicine Man. She can't be in the car with you and your eyes cannot meet hers until the rites have been performed—even though she knows you are not Zia's sister, she has to adhere to this because the taboo affected her spirit also. So, sit here with your head down and don't look at her. Understand?"

"Yes."

This is all so weird, she thought.

"Okay, keep your head down until I tell you otherwise. I don't even want her to see you in the rear-view mirror. Although, I'm sure she won't look."

Eventually, they pulled up to the hogan of Hosteen Begay and parked. Selene kept her head down until Ben told her that Anjelah had entered the hogan, where Zia would be sitting at the feet of the Medicine Man. Ben waited outside until he was summoned.

Selene sat there for at least an hour, wondering what to expect next. Finally, Ben came out and got into the car.

"What's going on, Dad?"

"Hosteen Begay will perform the Night Chant for Zia and his mother together to restore their mental and spiritual health. They will finish at dawn."

"How is Zia, Dad?"

"Quiet."

"Did you tell him I'm not his sister?"

"The hand trembler had already sensed that and asked to see

me."

"So, what happened then?"

"I squatted in front of where he sat and he went into a kind of trance, then he passed his trembling hand over me again and again."

"Wow. What did he say?"

"Well, it was in Navajo, so I understood some. Angie explained that we all need the spiritual cleansing of a sweat bath. He knew you were here—he could feel your presence. He wants Zia, Angie, me, you and your mom to participate. This is the only way our families can be made whole again."

"The only way in the Navajo world, you mean. How does it work? When do we do it? What about Mom—do you think she'll go along with it?"

"You ask too many questions."

"We meet back here tomorrow at dawn after the Night Chant. You can see the sweat lodge from here—next to the hogan." He pointed toward it. We're supposed to try and fast for the rest of the day...and no alcohol or cigarettes, but we can drink water. Not smoking will be tough for me—especially today. We are also supposed to contemplate and meditate, if possible. That's something I've never done. I'll try, though.

For tomorrow, we have to wear loose, comfortable clothes and each bring a towel. No jewelry. No frills. And...a woman can't be on her moon, as they call it."

He glanced over at Selene and shrugged, a bit embarrassed.

"Her moon! I've never heard it called that. Well, for your

information, I'm not on my moon."

"Do you think Mom is still at the abuelita's?"

"I'd be gone from there if I were her."

"For sure," Selene chuckled.

"Let's head back to Gallup, Selene. We need to plan for tomorrow. They'll start the Night Chant at dusk. As far as I can remember, the Medicine Man asks the Holy People to be present while he identifies the patients and describes their expected transformation to renewed health. They sing the same chants all night long—strangely hypnotic, a kind of poetry—and the next thing you know its dawn."

"Have you been to one, Dad?"

"Not to a Night Chant. But remember, I grew up here and understand a lot of the customs. That's why I'm so willing to go along with the sweat bath. It just might help us."

"Well, I'm waiting to see Mom's face when we hit her with this one."

"You know something, Selene, she's in the deepest hole of all of us and probably needs the healing and cleansing the most."

***

A hint of pink dawn glowed on the horizon as they drove up to Hosteen Begay's hogan. Ben parked to the side, away from the east-facing door. He said they should sit in the car and wait. Cecelia seemed nervous, but Selene convinced her it was the right thing to do.

"The sweat house is over there next to the hogan, Cecelia" Ben pointed. "Hosteen Begay has helpers heating the rocks. They'll place them in the center pit inside."

Just as dawn arrived, Zia stepped out of the hogan toward the rising sun. He stood still and seemed to be in deep concentration. His mother appeared next and stood by him. Then Hosteen Begay walked out continuing his songful prayer. He gave each of them corn pollen from his pouch and they sprinkled it on their tongues between thumb and forefinger, then each touched the tops of their heads and released the remaining pollen dust from their fingers into the morning air toward the east.

"They're finished," Ben announced.

They turned and followed the Medicine Man back into the hogan.

"How long does this sweat bath take, Dad?"

"It takes as long as necessary—would be the Navajo answer. I did the sweat bath a few times in high school, so I'll try to explain it. First is the purification. All sense of race, color, religion and gender disappear so that we are seen as equals to the Creator. When the steam and temperature begin to rise, strangely, your senses rise along with it, because Navajos believe the Spirit World senses the consciousness of the group. A talking stick will be passed to each of us—then one at a time, we'll each have a chance to speak, to pray, to ask for guidance from the Creator and the people we have hurt."

"Sounds like we really do need this, Dad...but I'm kind of scared."

Selene leaned forward touching the back of the passenger seat. "What about you, Mom?"

"I think I might stay in the car."

"No way!" Ben said turning toward Cecelia. "You're doing this."

"Can't I just go to confession…talk to a priest or something?"

"NO!"

The Medicine Man walked out of the hogan followed by Zia and Anjelah. Hosteen Begay was shirtless and wore light soft trousers and moccasins and had a kerchief wrapped at his forehead and tied at the nape of his neck. Zia was shirtless also. Anjelah wore her traditional clothing, a long skirt and loose tunic of light cotton fabric.

"Hosteen Begay is motioning us to come now. That's the prayer stick he's holding," Ben said.

Zia and Anjelah walked toward the sweat house.

"Dad, Zia didn't even look at us or acknowledge us."

"He's in a meditative state—not exactly a time to be waving greetings to us."

They each stepped out of the car into the chilly morning. Ben took his shirt off and pulled his wallet from his back pocket and dropped the shirt, wallet and car keys on the driver's seat. His belongings were safe there.

They tentatively walked toward the sweat house, each carrying a hand towel. Ben was first to stoop down and enter—giving himself time for his eyes to adjust. Walking clockwise, he sat on the dirt floor next to Zia and his mother, then crossed his legs and sat straight against the wall. Selene and Cecelia followed.

Interesting, Selene thought. The mothers are at either end of the group.

After they sat cross-legged on the floor, the Medicine Man looked from one to the other as if seeing into their souls—and signaled the doorkeeper to close the flap. Silence. Hosteen Begay gave the keeper a sign to open the flap again and bring in the red hot stones that they had heated in the sacred fire.

As Ben had explained earlier, the ceremony would begin when the Medicine Man sounded the Water Drum and prayed for the spirit guides from the four directions.

They watched as Hosteen Begay dipped water and poured it on the hot stones in the four directions, producing columns of steam. Then he began his prayers, songs and chants of purification.

Selene felt lightheaded and glanced sideways at her mother whose eyes were closed—hopefully in meditation or concentration. Maybe it was the hypnotic rhythms of the Navajo chant or the steam and the sweat, but something was happening in there. Selene could feel it.

After a long, dreamy silence, the Medicine Man said something in Navajo to Zia and handed him the talking stick.

"We are here to pray to the Creator and the Spirit People for the healing cleanliness and strength of honesty. I, Zia Yazzie, can claim that from this sunrise and onward—within the dual worlds in which I live—that Ben Monroe and Anjelah Yazzie are my biological parents, and that this truth will never be hidden from anyone again. I pray for guidance from the Creator for all of us."

Zia handed the talking stick to Ben, and Ben took Zia's lead in the tone of his statement.

"I, Ben Monroe, from this day forward will honor the truth that Zia Yazzie is my biological son—a man who thrives in his dual worlds, a man I am proud to call my son. I respect Anjelah Yazzie for being his caring and devoted mother. I regret not being a proper father to Zia and hope that I can learn to be. I pray for guidance from the Creator and acceptance from those I have hurt."

Ben handed the talking stick to Anjelah. Her voice was soft and melodic as she spoke in Navajo, then in English.

"I, Anjelah Yazzie, am the proud and humble mother of Zia Yazzie. I thank the Creator for the union with Ben Monroe that created our son. As his father, he has always been responsible in taking care of Zia, and he should be respected for that. From this dawn forward my hope is that in being a true father, Ben will understand and share in Zia's hopes, dreams and personal expectations. I pray for Mother Earth and Father Sky to guide them both."

Anjelah nodded toward Selene, and the talking stick was passed to her.

I feel an overwhelming sense of acceptance from Zia's mother, Selene thought.

"I, Selene Monroe, am not the person I thought I was—as though my identity was ripped away. From this day forward, I must accept the fact that Ben Monroe is not my biological father—although he is the only father I have ever known, and, therefore, I respect and honor him as such. I hope that he will continue to acknowledge me as his daughter. I'm trying to understand that what my mother did was motivated by protection of me. Complete forgiveness and understanding will take some time."

Selene handed the talking stick to her mother, whose head had been down through the entire ceremony. Before she began, she dabbed sweat from her face with the already damp towel.

"I," she stuttered. "I...Cecelia Aragon Monroe, have lived a lie for far too long. From this day forward, I share the truth that my daughter was conceived out-of-wedlock with a man who doesn't know he is her biological father. Her only *real* father is Ben Monroe. I ask forgiveness from Selene and Ben for my life of deceit and for how my dishonesty has hurt them...if forgiveness is possible."

Cecelia handed the talking stick to Ben.

"I, Ben Monroe, have not led a perfect life, and I accept my wife and will work toward complete forgiveness and a better life together. Nothing will change my feelings toward my daughter, Selene. Furthermore, as Angie suggests, I will strive for a better understanding of my son Zia's expectations for himself. I live with the strange irony that the daughter who is not of my blood calls me 'Dad' and that the son who shares my blood calls me 'Ben.'"

Ben handed the talking stick back to Hosteen Begay.

"Hozhó," he said, bowing his head.

The Medicine Man signaled for the flap to be opened, and one by one they left.

The morning chill refreshed them. Ben walked to the side of the sweat house followed by Selene and Cecelia. He filled a tin cup from a bucket of fresh water for them to share.

Zia and his mother followed the Medicine Man into the hogan.

When they reached the car, Ben quickly put his shirt on and grabbed his keys and wallet.

"I'll be back in a few minutes. I need to give Hosteen Begay some money for his services. It's hard for these medicine men. Sometimes the Navajos can only pay them in sheep, goats or jewelry."

***

Luz paced nervously across the kitchen floor and reached into her apron pocket for her rosary. She crossed herself and said a quick prayer for peace in the family and slipped the rosary back in place.

It's hardest to be the one waiting, she thought.

Well, she thought, I don't know about these pagan rituals, but I guess they are ingenious to our part of the world. One thing I know for sure is that everyone is going to come home hungry.

She got to work on a big pot of green chile stew—cubes of beef, onions, carrots, garlic and potatoes in a perfect gravy with diced green chile. She had thawed the chile—some of the remaining 40-pound sack they got from Hatch in the early fall. She had roasted and peeled it, then frozen it in small packages. What a chore. Her hands burned for days after from the spicy heat of the chiles, but green chile was a New Mexico staple.

While the stew simmered, she made two batches of dough—one

for tortillas, and one for sopaípillas—setting them aside. She rolled and patted tortillas and sizzled them on the cast-iron griddle. Later, she would roll out the dough for the sopaípillas and cut it into triangles. They would puff up when she fried them in the hot lard and served immediately—to be filled with honey and enjoyed.

Comforting food is what they need, she thought. "*Panza llena, corazón contenta*—a full stomach, a happy heart."

Luz paced again and fingered her rosary, praying once more for peace in the household.

She cringed as she heard the car pull up behind the house and quickly sat at the table pretending to be relaxed and enjoying her morning coffee.

Selene was the first to pop in the back door.

"Oh, Luz, it smells delicious in here," as she walked over and grabbed a pot holder to take a look. "Green chile stew. I'm starving."

Cecelia and Ben came in next. Luz didn't feel any animosity, and their auras seemed bright and content.

Hmm, maybe they have renewed their karma, Luz thought.

"I suppose you're both starving, too?"

They nodded in agreement.

"Okay then, *ándale*. Get washed up and then gather at the table. I'll start the sopaípillas. I want to hear everything that happened."

As they ate and talked they seemed to have a new unity and Luz felt forgiveness had at least begun.

Es un milagro, gracias a Dios, she thought. It's a miracle. Thanks God.

"I'm going to run upstairs and shower and go check on the store," Ben said. "I've got to make sure everything is in good order so I can go out to Thoreau tomorrow to talk to Zia—and probably stop and see my parents, too."

"I want to go with you, Dad."

"No, not this time."

PART 5: THE WHIRLING LOG OF LIFE

Red Cliffs Trading Post never changed, Ben thought as he parked next to his father's '54 Chevy pickup in front of the weathered store. The gravity-fed gas pumps stood empty and outdated. When I-40 bypassed Thoreau and Route 66, things slowed down. But, there was still business from travelers heading to and from Crownpoint, Chaco Canyon and Farmington.

The whole place remained locked in a 1950s time warp, Ben thought—knowing it was filled with cheap souvenirs, post cards and rickety showcases full of equally inexpensive Indian jewelry.

The front door squeaked on worn hinges when he opened it. His mother and father were sitting in their usual places behind the cash register—their startled looks told him it had been a while since he'd stopped by.

"Lord a mercy, Ben, how surprisin'," his mother said. She walked from behind the showcase and gave him a big hug.

"It's good to see you, Momma."

"How have you been, Daddy?" he asked, reaching across the showcase to give his father a hearty handshake.

"Fair to middlin', son. Tarnation, what brings you around?"

"Guilt, I guess," Ben said shoving his hands in his pockets. "I know it's been way too long since I visited. You know me, work, work, work."

They looked old and tired to Ben. His mother wore a threadbare housedress and a lumpy sweater, and his father's worn-out denims were held up by ratty suspenders.

"What about you two, don't you ever leave this place?"

"Naw, you know me and Momma, we just work it every day, like you, work, work, work."

"Come on back to the kitchen, Boy, and Momma will put some coffee on the stove."

If the store was locked in the '50s, the living quarters at the back of the building were the same as when he was a child. A cracked oilcloth covered the small kitchen table and the room was dark with old worn metal cabinets and nearly disappearing countertops. He watched his mother fill the speckled metal pot with water and light the propane stove with a wooden match. From the canister of coffee, she was ready to toss in the grounds at the right moment—add a little cold water to let them settle, then ladle out coffee into tin mugs. She set a tin of biscuits on the table and reached for a jar of homemade preserves.

"Do you still eat bologna sandwiches for lunch every day?"

"Yep, pretty much. But Momma still plants her garden in the summer."

"Daddy, why don't you take Momma out for a nice dinner sometime? There's a steakhouse in Grants now. You could have a T-bone, a baked potato and a salad with blue cheese dressing. That's what everyone else does. You can afford it. Don't just stash all that money. Let go of a little now and then."

Ben wondered how much money his father had hidden around there.

"Um, Daddy, that sounds good," his mother's eyes lit up as if that steak dinner might be a first for her.

"How's my beautiful granddaughter doing?" his mother asked beaming.

"Good. She's in college now and living in Albuquerque at the abuelita's house. She's home for spring break until tomorrow."

"Did she do anything special?"

"Not really."

Oh, he thought, it was life-changing, and hopefully you'll never know about it, and I will never tell you the truth about her.

"My, my, how the years just slip away," she whispered, looking lost in her time warp.

Ben munched on a stale biscuit mounded with jam to soften it a bit and sipped on campfire-style coffee. There wasn't much left to talk about. His parents' lives were a carbon copy of each and every day that passed.

"Well, I have to be going now. I have some business to take care of in the area, and I'm glad I got to see you both. Drive into Gallup, and I'll take you out to lunch or dinner. It would do you both good to take a day off now and then."

"I'll tell Selene you were asking for her."

Ben kissed his mother on the cheek and shook his father's hand once again. It felt strange to have such distance between them—but that's the way it had always been. Maybe that's why he didn't know how to be a father to Zia. Maybe he could learn.

The quick ride to Anjelah's hogan didn't give him much time to figure out what to do next—he didn't really have a plan.

The old blue pick-up sat out front with the small trailer holding the water tank attached. Zia must have filled the tank with water for his mother. Wood was chopped and stacked at one corner of the eight-sided dwelling. Zia's work, no doubt.

Anjelah opened the door when she heard the car and motioned for Ben to come inside.

Both Zia and Anjelah stared at Ben in silence.

"I don't know where to begin," he said, shrugging his shoulders and spreading palms open in a questioning gesture. "What do we do now?"

"We have to do something, but I don't know what it is either, Ben," Zia answered. "White people are always in a hurry. I feel like I've been in the middle of a racing, twisting dust devil. Maybe we need time for the whirlwind to unwind so we can see what the universe is telling us."

"Well, I suppose you're right, Zia. What do you think, Angie?"

"While the ill winds settle, we must be peaceful and thoughtful and allow the air to breathe new life into us. Then we will know what to do."

"I agree. I have a lot to consider, too, and I don't want to make any bad suggestions or have selfish expectations. We'll talk again in a few days. I'll be back."

Ben left knowing he had to respect their suggestions, but thought, dammit, I have a business to run while the universe figures this out.

***

Matthew Monroe paced the creaking wood floor of Red Cliffs Trading Post, thinking about what his son, Ben, had said. They did need to get away, but he hated to leave his money. For years and years he had stuffed wads of bills in hiding places everywhere in the store and the shed. What if someone broke in? What if there was a fire? Then again, what if he dropped dead?

Even Melba didn't know where he had it all hidden—in pockets of coats hanging in the closet, behind framed pictures, in shoe boxes, in files. He even kept a stash in one of the canvas water bags he used to sell tourists in case their radiators overheated. Years earlier, he had built a safe out of an old propane tank and had it nearly filled with 20-dollar bills and secured in the shed.

Yes, he could afford to take his wife, Melba, to dinner in Grants and treat her to a big steak. And it might be time to drive to Gallup and see Ben's store, too. They hadn't been anywhere in years, and the old Chevy pick-up needed a good run. The only place he'd driven it was to the market in Thoreau, the Baptist church and the dump.

Besides, he thought, I'm dog-tired…can't even breathe good no more. Maybe it's time to retire and buy a trailer house in Gallup or Grants.

Tuesday, he decided. Yes, it would have to be Tuesday when they went to dinner in Grants. They couldn't leave the store this weekend. Sunday was church and Bible study before they opened the store, and Monday was his day to do bookkeeping—*The King is in the counting house, counting all his money.* Tuesday would be their big outing.

***

Zia sat on the bench under the piñon tree in front of the hogan and stared out toward Mt. Taylor in the distance, trying to make sense of all that had happened in the past few days. He felt drained and exhausted. At least the truth was out about him. Then there was the shock about Selene—she wasn't his sister and wasn't Ben's daughter—but it still felt eerily strange, like she really was his sister,

179

and he was afraid to go anywhere near her.

He knew Ben Monroe well enough to recognize that Ben wanted him to return to Gallup immediately. Ben had no patience with the universe.

Zia closed his eyes and allowed his thoughts to flow freely in the four directions. He saw the ancient symbol of the whirling log— spinning counterclockwise, representing the circle of life and the four seasons. He concentrated on the balance that had been returned to his life and focused on his future and the reality that was his current life.

Choosing to spend the next few days working on his independent study, Zia relished the quiet and the ability to give his ideas complete freedom and concentration.

He decided his next presentation on the Navajo Arts and Crafts Academy would be strongly curriculum-based with sample courses of study. He was tired of the dean's ridicule. He thought of things he'd like to tell him to his face...thing like, you insult me about applying for grants when "the university" gets grant money for scientific studies on drought and rat poop. Anthropologists study the "history" of our ancient Anasazi people crossing the Bering Strait, but you think what I want for my people—here and now—is outrageous. You think all I should be doing is teaching arithmetic to Indians.

Zia was fired up with enthusiasm. He ducked inside the hogan and grabbed a notebook and pen from his knapsack, then went back outside to sit on the bench and get to work. Feeling inspired, his vision for the Navajo Arts and Crafts Academy was strengthened.

Zia outlined his concept and ideas flew onto the pages of his notebook.

***

"Momma, we're closin' early today and goin' inta Grants and do some shoppin' and have us a steak dinner at that restaurant Ben told us about," Matthew said, putting his thumbs behind the suspenders at his waist.

"That sounds mighty nice to me, Daddy."

They closed the store around three o'clock. The old truck puttered along Route 66 as cars zoomed past them.

"Ya know, momma, I'm getting purty tired anymore. I'm thinkin' we oughta retire—maybe get us a trailer house."

"Well, Daddy, I think that's somethin' real good for us to talk about while we're havin' our steak dinner."

Closer to Prewitt, Matthew gasped and slumped over the wheel. Melba screamed and slid across the seat trying to right the pickup, but they were hit by an on-coming logging truck and sent careening into the rocky landscape. Their truck rolled and smashed. Doors flew open. Matthew and Melba were thrown out like rag dolls and crushed against the earth.

***

"So that's the whole story, Louise." Ben took the last drag on his cigarette and stubbed it out in the ash tray on his desk.

"Well, Ben, I'm speechless. What did you tell Jerry?"

"I just told him that Zia is my son. Nothing else. No big deal to him, all he cares about is his commission."

Ben rolled his chair back, stood up and clapped his hands together.

"Okay, Louise, I'm exhausted from all this drama. It's time to close up and go home."

Just as he walked out of the office, the Chief of Police trudged into the store.

"Hey, why the long face, old buddy?"

"Ben? Oh, Jesus...I don't know how to tell you this."

He fumbled around with his keys, took off his hat, checked for his gun.

"What? What happened?" Ben's mind reeled in terror before his friend even spoke.

"Ben...it's your folks. They were in a terrible car accident coming into Prewitt," he said putting his head down like he dreaded his next words.

"We just got the call, and I wanted to tell you myself, Ben. They were both killed."

"No. No. God, no!"

"I'm so sorry, Ben," his friend said, putting his hand gently on Ben's shoulder.

Ben went ashen. He tried lighting a cigarette, but his hands were shaking.

Louise ran out of the office, sensing that something terrible had happened.

"What's wrong?"

"Ben's folks were killed in a car accident a couple of hours ago in Prewitt. I think he's in shock. Can we go sit in the office—maybe get him a glass of water...or whiskey?"

Ben slumped into his chair. Louise brought him the water and moved her chair over close to him and motioned for the Chief of Police to sit with Ben.

"Tell me everything," Ben insisted, lighting the cigarette with his trembling hands.

"I'll tell you what I know. Their pickup veered into oncoming traffic and they were hit by a logging truck, and their vehicle rolled several times. They were thrown out."

"Oh, no! It's all my fault! I was just there the other day and told them to go to Grants and have a steak dinner—not sit in that store eating bologna sandwiches every day. Oh God!"

"You can't blame yourself, Ben. Wait. Wait. There's more to the story. The car behind them was closing in, waiting to pass and said he saw the driver slump over and the passenger lean across the seat and try to steer the truck."

"Do you think maybe my father had a heart attack or something?"

"We don't know yet. The driver of that car went directly to the nearby trading post to call police. The owner jumped in his truck and raced to the scene to help—but it was too late. He immediately recognized the pickup and your parents and waited for the police and ambulances to arrive. When they identified them, he told police that you were their son, and they called us."

"Yes, that's Dave Ortega from Zuni Mountain Trading Post. We've known him for years."

"Ben, drink some more water and take these aspirins," Louise said softly, putting the aspirins next to the glass of water. "I can't begin to tell you how sorry I am."

The Chief of Police stood up.

"Ben, I need you to go with me to Grants to identify the bodies and authorize an autopsy on your father. Can you handle it?"

"I have to handle it."

He lit a cigarette.

"Ben, call Cecelia and tell her. This is awful news, and she'll have to let everyone know."

***

The next few days were a blur for Ben—a mind-numbing, nauseating blur. Confirmation that his father had had a massive heart attack didn't diminish his guilt.

Cecelia took over funeral plans, picked out coffins at the mortuary in Grants and arranged for the service at Matthew and Melba's Baptist church in Thoreau. Ben gave her a check for a healthy donation to the church, and the ladies auxiliary volunteered to serve a pot-luck luncheon in the church hall after the burial service at the small local cemetery.

The tragic accident had been covered by the Grants and Gallup newspapers and the Monroe family was flooded with sympathy and condolences.

By the time the funeral procession arrived from Grants, the small church had filled with mourners. Flowers arrangements jammed the area behind the podium.

Anjelah and Zia Yazzie stood outside. They waited to pay their respects to Ben and the family. Funerals like this were not their custom, but they knew they had to attend. The news of the tragedy was everywhere in the area.

"Zia…Angie…thank you for coming," Ben said as he got out of the black limo.

"We feel so bad, Ben. My mother and I wanted to see you before we went in for the funeral."

"Stay right here. You're walking in with us—sitting with the family."

Cecelia and Selene slid out of the limo next, both dressed in black. Zia walked over to them, knowing he couldn't stop thinking and dreaming about Selene.

"Hello, Cecelia. Selene, I'm really sorry for the loss of your grandparents."

"Zia, they are *your* grandparents."

"You're right, but I really didn't know them. You did. So I see them as *your* grandparents."

They stood and stared deep into each other's eyes looking for some signal—some sign to move forward.

Cecelia greeted Anjelah and the two mothers joined Zia and Selene. Ben took one last puff of his cigarette and readied himself for the service as he looked at his unique family.

Zia doesn't know that he was mentioned as their grandson in the obituary, Ben thought.

***

The drive to Thoreau had become a daily dose of mourning and guilt for Ben. He barely noticed the sandstone cliffs standing solid and strong as he drove up to Zia's hogan. Zia sat on the bench outside writing in a notebook.

"Zia, Selene is staying home for the rest of the week. I want the two of you to help me at my folks place...to go through things. I don't know where to begin."

"But, Ben, what about *chindi?*"

"They didn't die there, Zia. Their spirits aren't there."

"I can only trust you and Selene with this. You see, my father hid money all over that place. We have to go through everything. I don't even know if he had a will."

"Are you sure you want to do this so quickly, Ben? You look awful."

"Well, I feel awful, but it's got to be done."

"Okay. When?"

"I'll pick you up tomorrow morning at about 9 o'clock."

Ben trudged to his car, thinking of his mother's purse and father's wallet and keys sitting on the passenger's seat—all he had left of them after sending them to their death. He dreaded tomorrow.

***

Just before 9 a.m., a cloud of dust announced the arrival of Ben in his big blue Lincoln, but another cloud of dust followed—an older model large maroon-colored Lincoln. As they got closer, Zia saw that Selene drove the second car. Hmm, he thought. What's that about.

Zia let the dust settle before he opened the door, while Selene and Ben parked and got out of the cars.

"Dad, am I allowed to go in this time?"

"Of course, but follow me and do as I do. There is a protocol here."

Selene followed Ben's lead and once inside, close to the wood stove, Anjelah offered to make coffee.

"That's not necessary, Angie."

"Selene, will you give me those keys," Ben asked.

Selene dropped the car keys in Ben's palm.

"Angie, I have this extra car that I want you to have."

As he handed her the keys, she stepped back and clasped her hands behind her back.

"Don't even try to refuse this, Angie. You need a dependable car to go to Gallup and shop and visit Zia…whatever you need to do. It's yours. Now take the keys."

She stepped forward shyly and he took her hand and placed the keys in her palm.

"Thank you, Ben."

"There, was that so bad?" Ben laughed. Selene and Zia stood by quietly.

"Thanks, Ben. My mother really does need a car. The old truck is good for hauling water and wood, but not for a road trip of any kind. It's going to take some getting used to—it's big."

Selene grinned and said, "It's a tank."

Anjelah covered her mouth and giggled.

"Okay," Ben clapped his hands. "We've got work to do. You can drive over and visit us if you want to get some practice, Angie."

They piled into Ben's car, not knowing what was ahead of them at Red Cliffs Trading Post, but they were the only ones for the job.

When they walked in, Selene marched through the store and living quarters and came back carrying a framed photo.

"Zia, look at this picture of Dad when he was a kid. It looks exactly like you. It's in this ratty old frame with broken glass. I'm taking it out so you can see it better," Selene said. "It's Dad. But it's you."

As Selene dismantled the frame to get to the photo, four $100 bills fell out.

"Dad was right. There's money hidden in weird places around here. But look at this picture, it's you!"

Zia stared at the photo for a long time.

"I guess I'm a Navajo Ben Monroe."

"It sure looks like it."

Zia stared at the picture again. He had never seen photographs of his family. Navajos thought photos captured their spirit. He knew he resembled Ben but couldn't believe that he looked exactly like him—only the Navajo version.

"Where's Dad? I have to show this to him."

"I think he's out in the shed."

Zia continued going through files, putting aside anything that looked important and finding money. He didn't want to touch their clothes in the closet or look through drawers in the dresser. That was too close to chindi for him.

Ben worked diligently in the shed. A pile of things to take to the dump sat outside, and in the corner he arranged tools and fixtures he could donate to the church rummage sale. Then he hit the mother lode—the propane tank. He was digging cash out when Selene ran in.

"Oh, my God, that's a huge pile of money! Look, I just found four one-hundred dollar bills in an old picture frame with this photo." She handed it to him.

"That's me…but it looks like Zia…amazing." He stared at it for a long time, then handed it to Selene. "Give this to Zia to take to his mother."

"Okay, back to work, Selene. Get a box—a big one—and put all this cash in it, then take it to the kitchen table and, neat and orderly, put in bundles of $500—then wrap each bundle with a rubber band. There has to be rubber bands somewhere."

Selene gaped at all the cash and shook her head. "Okay, I'll be right back."

On the file folder tab "WILL" was hand-written. Zia didn't open the folder, but pulled it out to take to Ben and bumped right into Selene coming in the back door. They stopped and stared long and deeply at each other.

"What do *we* do now, Zia? About us?"

"I don't know. I think we have to wait for the universe to tell us, Selene."

Selene put her hands on her hips and stepped back and looked upward into the vast blue sky. "Hmm, the universe? Maybe you're right. I sure can't figure it out," she shrugged and walked into the store.

Zia held onto the file and stepped into the shed to see the pile of cash.

"Wow, Ben. Didn't your dad believe in banks?"

"Guess not."

Zia handed the folder to Ben.

"Here's a file I just found that says 'Will.' I didn't open it."

Ben took the folder, and Zia turned and walked back toward the house passing Selene holding a giant box.

Zia glanced up to into the clear blue sky. Come on, universe!

While Selene piled cash into the large box, Ben walked into the kitchen and sat at the table to read the will.

Written in his father's hand, the will stated that should Matthew pre-decease Melba, everything would go to her and vice-versa. Upon the death of the surviving spouse, everything would go to any heirs of their son, Ben Monroe.

Ben dropped the folder on the table. "The heirs," it read. That means they never forgot about Zia, he thought.

Ben put his head in his hands—a new surge of guilt raged

through him. It was his fault they never knew Zia. He should have brought his son around. They could have had a relationship with their grandson. That was my responsibility. They were simple, God-fearing people who didn't want to interfere.

How much more self-loathing can I take?

Ben closed the folder, lit a cigarette, then stood up and paced across the kitchen. A long ash fell to the floor without his notice. Should he tell Zia and Selene now?

Zia held a new stack of important folders and set them on the kitchen table.

"Ben, I found a few more folders that you should see. One says 'Deeds,' the other 'Banking.' This one fell open when I pulled it out. It says 'Past Due Bills,' and it's full of $2 silver certificates. I think your father had a sense of humor."

Selene lumbered in the back door with a packing box full of cash. Zia ran over, grabbed it from her and set it on the floor next to the table.

"I've never seen anything like this, Dad! I need another box. What are you going to do with all this money?"

"For starters, I just read the will and none of it is mine."

"What? That's impossible, Dad!"

Ben put his cigarette out and told Zia and Selene to pull up chairs at the table for the reading of the will. "This will was hand-written by Daddy in 1971. By then, Momma and Daddy knew I didn't need their money."

"Okay, now here's the part that's important. 'Upon the death of the surviving spouse, all of our worldly possessions shall become the property of any heirs of our son, Ben Monroe.'"

Ben looked from Zia to Selene. "That's the two of you."

Zia registered shock, and Selene just stared at Zia, smiling. "The universe is being very kind to you, Zia."

"I can't accept anything like this. It's not right," Zia grimaced. "They didn't intend this for me, Ben. I never even knew them."

"That's my fault, Zia. They knew about Angie and about you. Obviously, they never forgot about you."

"I'm the one who shouldn't get anything, Zia."

Ben stood up and paced, running his hand through his hair.

"My folks always stressed unconditional love. Their will is certainly proof of that. So you both better deal with it!"

He pulled a cigarette from the pack and before putting it in his mouth to light it, pointed to Zia then to Selene.

"Think about unconditional love…learn the lesson…and try to live it. For now, get back to bundling those twenties, Selene. And, Zia, back to the files."

Ben walked toward the front door.

"I'm going to that greasy spoon by the market to get us some lunch. Keep working."

"Boy, our dad is a real slave driver," Selene said winking at Zia. He winked back at her—both knowing Ben heard the remark.

Ben grinned as he walked outside—the first time he had smiled in days.

***

Ben lugged the heavy suitcase through the front door of the store, heaving it forward with both hands. Louise pushed her desk chair back quickly, stood and walked into the store.

"What do you have in that huge piece of luggage? It looks like a trunk."

"Money. I want to keep it in the vault. I'll explain everything in a minute. Whatever you do, don't tell Jerry anything. How is Fred holding up?"

"Actually, he's doing fine. He loves being here."

Ben strode out to the car and brought in the bulging canvas water bag.

"I remember those—haven't seen one in years. What's in it?"

"Money. I want you to help me with this, Louise," Ben asked as he carried it toward the office.

He plunked it down next to her desk—against the wall where it wasn't visible from the store—then he took out his pocket knife and slit the top to reveal an array of folded bills.

"I need you to count this. We have those wrappers from the bank, don't we?"

"Sure, I have them right here in my desk with the deposit books."

"Now, if you have a few minutes, sit down and I'll fill you in on all of this."

Louise nearly fell into her chair in amazement. Ben told her of the last few days at his folks' store—the money, the will.

"We've gone through everything. We're donating all the merchandise to the Baptist church auxiliary for their annual rummage sale. They should be able to raise a nice amount of cash for the church. That's the least we can do for the years my folks belonged there."

Louise nodded her head in agreement.

"How is Zia with all of this?"

"It's difficult for him," Ben paced and pulled a cigarette from his pack of Marlboros and lit it.

"Things have changed drastically for all of us…so quickly. I feel like a different person myself. Zia rode into Gallup with Selene and me yesterday afternoon. I wanted him to get his truck back so he could meet the church ladies at the store tomorrow to help them load up all the merchandise."

"Is he ever coming back to work?"

"We talked about that. He said he needed another day to work on his school project."

"Tell him I'll type it for him." She leaned forward. "Did he explain it to you? I'm so impressed with his ideas."

"Yes, we talked about it the entire trip back from Thoreau. Selene kept interrupting, asking questions, and making suggestions—in general, championing his cause. I told him I wanted to read every section of the proposal. I was impressed with his concept—especially the retail part of it."

"Like father, like son," Louise laughed.

***

Sunrise. The tangerine dawn swept across the enormous sky ahead of Zia. Deep breaths of the chilly spring air filled his lungs. The stillness quieted his mind long enough to distance himself from those whirlwinds the universe had tossed him lately.

One more day to work on his independent study was all he needed, then back to Gallup. Selene would be gone. Selene.

He couldn't stop thinking about her. What will happen with Selene? Has she been relegated to a sister? Is that the only relationship we can have now—brother and sister, even though we aren't? I don't think the sunrise or the universe can solve this puzzle easily.

Zia turned away from the bright sphere of sunshine and watched puffs of juniper pollen rise into the spring air, and stepped into the hogan to join his mother for coffee. He had talked to her at length about his surprise inheritance, and her reaction was like his—awkward.

He drove down to the old trading post and stood there alone, waiting for the ladies from the church. He looked at everything in a different light now. The place was run down and needed work. It sat on five acres, had easy access to I-40, old Rt. 66 and the state route at Thoreau that went on to Crownpoint, Chaco Canyon and Farmington.

Then, an idea struck him. What if this could be the beginning of The Navajo Arts and Crafts Academy?

It would take time and work and money, he thought. Soon, he would have some money. Well, not enough money, and nothing good happens fast anyway. But, he had no right to make these plans or explore these ideas without Selene. What would she say?

What would the dean say? Zia could almost hear the dean laughing at him. Maybe his ridicule fuels me more than anything, he thought. I would like to prove to him that my aspirations are more than just an independent study, a thesis or a dissertation—those bound copies of the lonely works of graduate students that sit piled up gathering dust. I won't do it that way. I have to follow my dream, even if I fail miserably. Well, "no guts, no glory" is what Ben always says.

***

Zia took a deep breath and strolled into the conference room for his presentation, realizing how much he had grown over the past few months. My thinking was more linear before—nothing abstract or creative, he thought. My experiences with Ben Monroe have broadened my viewpoints. I guess I should admit that to him.

"Mr. Yazzie, it's time for your dog-and-pony show," the dean said. "What do you have for us this time?"

"Curriculum," Zia stated, as Dr. Ortiz's assistant passed out the copies.

"Okay, if everyone can take a look at their copy, we can begin," she smiled, trying to change the mood of the meeting. "Zia, would you like to talk about the concept?"

"Yes, Dr. Ortiz. As you see, it's a strict and aggressive curriculum concentrating on solid basic education and balanced and reinforced by Navajo tradition and language."

"So, Mr. Yazzie," the dean questioned. "How are you going to get staff, students and parents to sign this contract you talk about here and make a commitment to your lofty ideals? "Let's see," he read from the proposal, 'Integrity, excellence in academic pursuit, self-discipline.' Are you serious?"

Zia gritted his teeth...then turned toward the dean. "The only way the concept can be successful is with that level of commitment. It's not easy—nothing worthwhile is easy—and this is a commitment to a better future for my people, and I think a contractual agreement is necessary.

Zia leaned forward and turned the page of the proposal.

"As you see, our day will start at 7:30 and end at 4:30 and will include lunch. If a student needs tutoring, we'll provide it. They don't move on until they learn, because this concept has a purpose. Parents have to agree to monitor their child's daily homework and limit distractions. Parents are an integral part of this concept—they are responsible—and we will hold regular meetings with parents. Students will wear uniforms."

"I know this is a silly question," Dr. Ortiz asked, "But, what will the uniforms look like?"

"I'm not sure yet," he said. "I don't really want our students to look like White kids from some Catholic school, but I do think uniforms create a more serious attitude."

"Well, I still say it's a lot of hooey," the dean said.

You arrogant honky, Zia thought.

"Your curriculum does look rigorous," the department chair said. "And, I must say, I rather approve of it, and the Navajo tradition and language section is well-structured. Overall, I think you've made amazing progress on this, Mr. Yazzie."

"Thank you, sir. I'm hoping to personalize or sort of customize their education—encourage them to think."

"What will you do next," the dean asked, "figure out a new way of counting sheep?"

Zia felt his ears burning and his heart racing and he blurted out, "Of course. We'll teach them to count all the legs and then divide by four!"

Dr. Ortiz jumped at the chance to conclude the session before the dean could interject more of his derision.

"Zia, we're getting closer to the end of the semester. You only have two more presentations, and then the committee will decide on your graduation."

"I understand, Dr. Ortiz."

Zia stood and left the conference room, now familiar with the procedures.

Ramona Ortiz stood up, planted her hands on her hips and stared at the dean. "Harry, I just don't understand why you are so hard on Zia. Why?"

"I'm wondering that, too," the department chair said.

"Calm down, you two," the dean said. He took off his glasses and set them on the table and looked from the department chair to Ramona Ortiz.

"What I see in that young man is something remarkable—something I haven't seen in years, and I'm really enjoying it. Every time I challenge him, he comes back with something better. He is a strategic, futuristic thinker with the good of his people as his goal. As you know, I'm the chairman for the annual graduation Innovation Award, and if Zia Yazzie can produce two more outstanding presentations, I will submit his name and his project to the committee and become his biggest advocate. Honestly, I think he could even win the national award with the strength of his concept."

The department chair smacked his fist on the conference table. "Dammit, Harry, you had me fooled."

Ramona Ortiz wiped away tears—and beamed.

***

Zia walked from the conference room. The dean is downright vindictive, he thought. What if he tries to sabotage me and I can't graduate? I've got to make these last two presentations better than ever. Persevere, persevere.

Zia strolled outside and took in a deep breath of cool spring air. He automatically began walking toward the Frontier. Would Selene be there?

When he saw Selene, his heart fluttered, and he wove through the crowd to where she sat.

Instead of a bright smile, a look of terror spread across her face.

"Zia, there's David Stanfield—my—my *real* father. He's walking this way. Can we get out of here? I'll drive us somewhere else. I'm parked outside."

She gathered her things quickly, and they squeezed through the crowded restaurant.

"Excuse me," he said, touching her elbow. "Aren't you Cecelia Aragon's daughter?"

So close to the door, she thought. Dammit. Almost made it.

Selene turned around.

"Yes… ah, yes, I am."

"We met a while back," he said. "Do you have time for coffee?"

"No, sorry. We were just leaving."

David Stanfield followed them outside and reached into the pocket of his corduroy jacket for his business card. "Could you give this to your mother and have her call me?" he said, staring at Selene as if examining her.

"How old are you?" he asked.

"Almost 20."

"Didn't your mother ever tell you about me?"

She shifted her books to her left arm and held them against her waist at the elbow.

"Uh…no, not until the day we met you here. She said you had dated while she went to school here. She said the abuelita didn't approve of you because you were older and a gringo."

Stanfield burst into laughter.

"Is the abuelita still around?"

"Yes, I live with her now while I'm going to UNM."

That voice—Selene's voice—is identical to my mother's, he thought.

"What are you studying?"

"Education. But that's not for me," she said, turning her right hand over with her palm facing up. "No… not for me."

My mother's hand gestures, he thought. Exactly. That's what she does when she wants to get her point across.

Zia piped up. "She asks so many questions, I told her she should be in journalism."

"Selene, we have to be going," Zia said as he took her hand and walked toward the car.

***

David Stanfied had lost his appetite. He wandered back to his office in a daze convinced Selene was his daughter.

The first time he heard her voice—it stunned him—sounded the same as his mother's. That's why he had left so quickly that day, making an excuse that he had a class in a few minutes. He was shaken by the possibility that she was his daughter. Now, he knew she was. Even though she looked like Cecelia, he could see his mother's elegance in her expressions and mannerisms—Victoria Vance Stanfield, the wealthy New York philanthropist.

Why didn't Cecelia ever tell me, he wondered? She just disappeared.

It seems so long ago, he thought. Well, I was full of myself in those years—a spoiled rich kid who came out west to be independent. I thought I could do anything and have anyone. Cecelia had to know I was fooling around on her, too. Now look at me— alone, never married, no children. Except Selene, if she's really my daughter.

***

The café at Duran's Pharmacy was packed, as usual. They sat at the counter and watched an endless number of tortillas sizzle and puff up on the grill for waiting customers.

"Well, Selene, it looks like you might have to do another sweat bath—this time with David Stanfield," Zia proposed.

"NO!"

"As one bastard child to another, I can tell you that you have to resolve this. You can't hide behind Ben Monroe when David Stanfield is your biological father. Nothing will ever compromise your love for Ben, but you owe it to yourself and Stanfield to tell him the truth. You're the daughter. The relationship is between you and him."

"Who died and left *you* boss?"

"I'll go with you if you want. Finish your green chile, and we'll go see David Stanfield. The universe is calling. Do it."

Selene sulked.

"Will this ever end?"

"No," Zia insisted. "Not until you are truthful."

"Why do have to be so damned honorable, Zia?"

"Well, if you knew what the universe was suggesting to me about you right now, you might not call me so damned honorable."

Selene put her head in her hands and shook with laughter.

"Okay, we'll go see David Stanfield."

She tore off a section of tortilla and scooped up a big helping of green chile with it...

"Here's to the universe"... then popped it in her mouth.

They drove back to the campus and headed for the journalism department. At the office, Selene asked for David Stanfield.

"These aren't his usual office hours to see students," the woman at the front desk answered.

"Please ask if he will see me. My name is Selene Monroe."

Within seconds David Stanfield was in the lobby ushering them into his office. Framed diplomas and awards covered the wall behind his desk. Shelves stood packed with books. He closed the door as they entered the office and offered Zia and Selene seats in front of his desk.

"What can I do for you?"

Zia began. "Selene has been through a lot lately, and her life isn't what she once thought. Do you want to explain, Selene?"

"Among the many shocks and surprises Zia and I have both had in the past few weeks is...

"Go ahead, Selene," Zia whispered.

"Is the fact that...that...well, I found out that you are my biological father."

"I knew it!" He jumped out of his chair.

Selene was taken aback by his enthusiasm, expecting rejection and disbelief.

David Stanfield sat, leaned forward and explained the feeling he had the first time he met Selene—how much she reminded him of his own mother—and why he left so abruptly. Today's accidental meeting confirmed his suspicions, and he said he had been sitting in his office trying to figure out how to approach Cecelia to find out the truth.

"Selene, this is all new to me. I've never married—never had a family…well, until now…until you. I don't have a clue how to be a father. I hope that there is a way we can have a relationship."

He shrugged his shoulders.

"I don't know how to go about it, but maybe there is a way. Can you try?"

"Yes, I'll try," Selene said.

"Selene, I am an only child, and my mother aches from never having grandchildren. You remind me so much of her, and I wish the two of you could meet. Do you think you could go with me to see her sometime?"

Selene squirmed nervously.

"I…I… I guess I could…maybe. Does she live here in Albuquerque?"

"No, New York."

"New York. I've never even been there. I don't know…."

"I'll take care of everything. I think she would be thrilled."

Selene fidgeted.

"I need some time to think about this. You're kind of impulsive."

"Gee, like somebody else I know," Zia laughed.

Selene had to chuckle. She actually liked David Stanfield.

She glanced out the office window, wondering what to do or say next, then looked at the name plate on his desk.

"Do I call you 'Dr. Stanfield? I see the Ph.D. here on your name plate."

"No, you call me 'David.' The Ph.D. stands for pile it higher and deeper."

She chuckled.

"Well, I think we've taken enough of your time for today." She stood to leave, then hesitated. "David…Ah, maybe we'll see you again. Like today…Zia and I meet every two weeks for lunch at the Frontier. Maybe we can start there."

"I look forward to it. I hope you'll begin to feel more comfortable about getting to know me and going to meet my mother."

"I'll try. I promise."

"When you leave, I'm going to call my mother and tell her about you. Is that okay?"

"Of course."

I still haven't had the heart-to-heart with my own mother, Selene thought. So much keeps happening, and we really, really need to have that conversation.

Selene and Zia walked from David Stanfield's office across

campus toward the parking lot.

"Now what do we do, Zia? All the skeletons are out of the closet," Selene said while sweeping her hands clean of the invisible quagmire.

"I'm not sure."

They strolled across campus passing students hurrying to class.

"The semester will be over soon, and Dad wants me to work in the store this summer. What do you think of that?"

"He told me that a while back, before I knew you were my sister—and then not my sister."

Selene rolled her eyes.

"You should come to Gallup this weekend and start your training. "I'll teach you everything I know."

Selene gave him a side glance. "What's that supposed to mean? And I'm not asking the universe anything."

Zia laughed. "Are you coming home this weekend or not?"

"Hmm, I guess so. Where's your truck parked?"

"Why? Are you in a hurry to get rid of me?" Zia said as he lifted his chin in the direction of the truck and moved his lower lip outward and made a puffing noise. "Choo."

"Just point it out," Selene said, impatiently.

"Selene, Navajos don't point."

"Oops. I should have remembered. Dad does that weird mouth pointing, puffing thing, too. You know, one minute you're a Navajo, then you're a belagaana. It's confusing sometimes, Zia."

With an easy transition into his Navajo accent, Zia said. "Just look at me like a combination plate."

"Yes, with green *chile* on top," Selene grinned, and gave Zia a quick kiss on the cheek and walked away.

PART 6: STERLING SOLUTIONS

As she drove to the abuelita's house, Selene tried hard to stem the flow of emotions that swept her in all directions. So much had happened so quickly; she felt like she had just stepped off the high speed roller coaster ride of a lifetime. So, if this is my new reality, she thought. I guess I'll have to deal with it.

She wondered what the abuelita would say when she explained her encounter with David Stanfield?

Inside the cozy adobe house, the tea kettle whistled, and the smell of cinnamon and anise wafted through the air from freshly-baked sweet, crumbly biscochitos. Selene walked to the kitchen and sat to talk to her great-grandmother.

"Selena, it's like you're living a *novela*, and you have to write the next chapter yourself. I can't help you. You have to trust your heart."

"You're right, Abuelita," she sighed, munching on a warm biscochito and sipping hot tea.

"Now I finally understand why you always say: 'It's a great life if you don't weaken!' "

"*Claro que sí, mijita.*"

"I've decided to allow David Stanfield in my life—maybe even go to New York and meet his mother," she sighed.

"Yes, I agree mijita. Besides, David Stanfield is a mature man now, not that *mocoso*—that snot that I remember from years ago."

They both laughed and sipped more tea. Selene felt less confused.

The abuelita is a wise woman, she thought, even if sometimes I'm afraid of what she's going to tell me.

"Since I'm working in my Dad's store this summer, I have to start training, so I'm going home this weekend to learn the ropes.

"Maybe while you're home you should talk to your mother about David Stanfield. I think she deserves to know and may have some advice for you."

"Yes, abuelita, you're right."

"I wonder if Mom ever met his mother."

The abuelita shrugged. "I don't know."

Selene washed her tea cup and snack plate in the hot soapy water that filled the sink, rinsed them, dried them and placed them in the cupboard—abuelita's rules.

Well, she thought, it might be enjoyable to spend the weekend in Gallup and start training in the store. Then there are the other possibilities....

Selene strolled to her room and opened the closet. What would she wear? First, she picked out a long-sleeved skinny-ribbed, navy turtleneck sweater and a pair of hip-hugger, bell-bottom slacks in a large plaid of sky blue, navy and gray. That would go nicely with her strings of turquoise heishi and the matching earrings. She had an array of silver bangle bracelets that would finish off the outfit. Next she selected a long-sleeved white blouse with a wide collar and large cuffs and a black midi-skirt with a wide belt. She could wear her boots with both outfits. She was set. She planned to get ready for "work" before she drove from Albuquerque early Saturday morning. She would surely wear makeup and even curl her hair with the hot rollers—but, the last thing she wanted was to look like one of those "Charlie's Angels" sorority girls.

*****

Luz sipped her morning coffee and wrote in a tablet, occasionally glancing at the latest issue of *New Mexico Magazine* that sat open on the kitchen table. She ripped out page after page from the tablet and crumpled one after another then tossed them onto the heap accumulating in front of her.

"What are you doing, Luz?" Cecelia asked as she walked in the kitchen toward the coffee pot.

"I'm writing a poem."

"Oh, I've never known you to write poetry."

"There's this contest," she said pointing to the magazine. "Whoever writes the best poem about chile will get it published in the chile harvest edition of *New Mexico Magazine* in the fall. The deadline is coming up, so I have to get it done."

"Can I read it?"

"No, not yet. I'm almost finished, though. I have a sick sense about these things."

She tapped the pencil to her forehead as if urging the right words out.

"I've got it," she wrote quickly.

After a few minutes, she put the pencil down. "Okay, CeCe, I'll read it to you. Are you ready?

Cecelia stifled a grin, not knowing what to expect, and winked at Ben who was about to walk into the kitchen, but instead quietly waited by the door.

"To outsiders, our favorite thing might sound silly,
But ask New Mexicans and we'll all say, 'Chile!'
From Chimayo to Mesilla Valley and Hatch,
Our reds and our greens are a fiery hot match.
We roast them and peel them and dry them to store,
And we can't go without chile for a day or more.
We decorate our porches with red chile strings,
And some ladies they wear red chile earrings.
We put chile in everything from eggs to posole,
It's only the tourists who eat guacamole."

Applause came from behind Luz as Ben strolled in, and Cecelia's delighted laughter filled the room. "'It's only the tourists who eat guacamole.' That's hilarious, Luz. I think you'll win!"

"Since when did you become a poet?" Ben asked.

"Since this morning. You know me, Señor Ben, I have a way with words."

Cecelia rolled her eyes at Ben and he chuckled.

"Cecelia, how about leaving our poet here with her creation, and you and I go out to breakfast?" Ben suggested.

"Great idea."

As they drove, Ben said, "We've been through a lot these past weeks, and we need some time together to re-establish our relationship. We can't just accept, accept, accept and go on in a fog."

"You're right, Ben. Everything has changed. What do we do, go to a marriage counselor or a priest?"

"No. If you and I can't make it right, no stranger can. Besides, Cecelia, I think you and I are connected by our own frailty and vulnerability."

Cecelia exhaled a huge sigh. "Ben Monroe, that's the most loving thing I've ever heard you say."

Ben gave her a quick, contented glance.

"I think we should go away for a weekend," Ben said. "How about someplace completely different, where we don't know anyone and can't be distracted...someplace where we can *really* establish a new relationship."

"I'm willing. I don't want to be in limbo anymore. I'd gladly reinvent *us*. Maybe all we've been through can make us better. We've been drifting for a while anyway. You know it and I know it—just existing. Maybe we still have hope. Our secrets have imprisoned us long enough."

They drove along Route 66 and pulled into the El Rancho Hotel.

"Here's where we started," Ben said. "You were waiting tables, and I was chasing dreams."

"Oh yes, where our eyes met like magnets. That was the worst line I'd ever heard, Ben."

"Now you tell me! Well, I'll never use that one again."

After breakfast at El Rancho, they stopped by the store before anyone was there. Ben took Cecelia into the vault to show her the stash of money from his parents' place.

"They lived so frugally. Who would have guessed they had this much money hidden?" she said.

"Well, it all belongs to Zia and Selene now," Ben said with a sweeping gesture toward the cash.

"Speaking of relationships, Ben, what do you think will happen with *them*?"

"Well, as Zia explains it, we'll have to leave that answer to the universe."

***

The store buzzed with business. Spring meant buying season for all the regional tourist attractions. Buyers arrived in Gallup to stock up for what they expected to be a banner season, with Indian jewelry being the rage.

Ben kicked into high gear. A parade of Navajo and Zuni artisans marched through the doors daily to sell him jewelry, and Ben had the vault and showcases packed. He concentrated on jewelry for his inventory surge—feeding the fashion frenzy. The vault filled up like a treasure trove for Ben. Hands on his hips, he stood admiring his inventory.

"Louise. Look at the fabulous jewelry that is being produced now," as he swept his hand toward the array in the vault. "It's like the artisans are meeting the challenge to outdo themselves…and succeeding. And, it's our opportunity to do more business."

That meant, he needed more manpower… or woman power, he thought. Maybe Cecelia could work in the store after all. She is good with people and a quick learner. And at least she's trustworthy. But, before the season begins, we need to work on us. We need that weekend vacation. Actually, this is the perfect weekend. Zia will be here to take over and so will Jerry and Selene. We could drive up to Santa Fe and stay in Tesuque at Rancho Encantado—that's a beautiful, quiet place—isolated from the business in Santa Fe that would definitely distract me. And, hopefully we could work on a new level of intimacy now that we're stripped of all our secrets and lies.

Ben stepped into the office and called home.

"Hello, Luz, is Cecelia anywhere close by?"

Cecelia's registered surprise at the fact that Ben was calling her at home. That rarely happened.

"Hi, Ben. Is everything okay?"

"Fine, fine. I was just wondering if you would like to work in the store. It's getting really busy. I know you mentioned it a few times, but I didn't take you seriously."

"Yes…Sure. I'd love to. When do I start?"

"How about tomorrow?"

"Okay."

She hung up the phone and turned and grinned at Luz.

"Guess what, Luz? I have a job."

"*No sé*, CeCe."

"Yes, Ben asked me to work in the store."

"That will be a great *excape* for you."

"I'm excited about it, Luz."

***

For her first day of work, Cecelia dressed in a black slacks and a blue silk blouse and wore the inlaid Charles Loloma bracelet Ben had given her for Christmas. Ben said the Hopi artisan was one of the best he had ever seen.

"Look," he said after she opened the gift. He took the 14K gold bracelet turned it over and pointed to the inlay that graced the underside. "This is what Loloma calls the soul of the piece. He says, like people—it's what's on the inside that makes them special."

This is the first time I've had the courage to wear this bracelet, she thought. Before, I never felt worthy of its significance.

Cecelia took a deep breath as she walked through the door of Monroe Trading Company—slightly nervous—for her first day of work.

"Hi Jerry. Did you hear that I'm your new co-worker?"

"Yes, Mrs. M."

"Please call me 'Cecelia'. I'm not your home room teacher. Actually, you have a lot to teach me."

"Okay, Mrs. M…I mean, Cecelia."

Jerry put out his cigarette and smoothed his hands together. "I'm ready whenever you are."

Zia stuck his head out of the vault. "Good morning, Cecelia. Glad you're going to be working with us."

Ben stepped out of the office. "Cecelia, come in here for a few minutes and fill out the payroll information for Louise."

"You're paying me?"

"Well, of course. It's a job; you should get paid."

Ben pointed toward Jerry. "Jerry can explain how the commission works."

While they sat in the office, Ben suggested they spend the weekend in Tesuque at *Rancho Encantado*. Louise could make the reservations.

"Wow, I just got the job and I already have a vacation."

"Enjoy it while you can. You're going to be on duty most weekends from now on."

"Okay, let's get to work," Cecelia said.

Still holding onto her purse, she walked toward Jerry.

"You can put your handbag on this shelf under the register, and we'll get started."

Ben lit a cigarette and walked into the vault.

"Zia, how does our inventory look?"

Zia ran his fingers through his hair while studying the merchandise.

"We're well stocked…except for high-end, collector's jewelry…especially Zuni."

"Actually, today would be a good day to go to Zuni," Ben suggested. "What do you think?"

Zia shrugged his shoulders. "Sure. Today would be fine."

Ben dug into his pocket and pulled out a wad of hundred dollar bills held with a Zuni inlaid silver money clip.

"Okay, I'll get the checkbook and some more cash from Louise."

Ben stopped short as he was walking out of the vault and turned around.

"Speaking of cash, when are you and Selene going to do something about this?" he said pointing to the giant old suitcase and taped-up water bag in the corner of the vault.

"Selene will be here this weekend to train in the store. We could decide then…maybe."

"Well, you better do something soon. You can't leave it sitting—"

"—Ben," Jerry interrupted. "Since it's early, could I show Cecelia how to ring up sales on the register?"

"Good idea. Then give those receipts to Louise so she can cancel them out.

"Will do."

Ben pointed his chin toward Zia. "We're going on a buying trip down to Zuni this morning, Jerry, so you and Cecelia are on your own."

***

Ah, Saturday morning. Zia opened the store…anxious. Louise wasn't working and Ben and Cecelia were away for the weekend. He'd have Selene to himself—except for Jerry.

Selene breezed into the store just as Zia opened the vault. When he turned, his eyes moved over every inch of her—all dressed up and looking gorgeous.

"Zia, you shouldn't stare at your sister that way," Jerry said.

Both Zia and Selene shot him a furious glance.

"Hey…hey, it's okay." Jerry crossed his hands in front of his face. "Cecelia gave me the scoop while you and Ben were in Zuni the other day."

"The scoop. What scoop?"

"Selene," Zia stopped her as she marched toward Jerry.

"Sorry, you guys. Let's start over. Your mother explained everything to me because she knew we would all be working together—the whole fam-damly."

"The whole fam-damly? Jeez, Jerry, don't you know when to stop?" Zia snapped.

Zia waved his hand signaling the end of the discussion.

"Let's get to work."

As much as Zia wanted Selene with him in the vault marking Zuni jewelry, he knew Jerry and Selene needed a truce and asked him to begin training her.

Selene was a quick learner and by the end of the day excelled as a new employee. She and Jerry even mended their earlier differences.

"Closing time, y'all," Jerry announced. "I'm going to stop for a cocktail. What about you two?"

"I think we'll get some dinner." Zia said and turned to Selene. "What do you think?"

"Yes, I'm overworked and hungry."

"You can go ahead, Jerry. I'll show Selene how to check out the drawer and we'll close the place up. See you tomorrow."

"Okay, later."

When the closing duties were finished, they walked outside to a beautiful evening.

"Can we walk somewhere, Zia? It's so nice out."

"Absolutely. There's a new Italian place along 66 across from the train depot. I've heard it's good. At least it's something different."

As they strolled to the corner, Zia took Selene's hand. "Does Luz know you're in town?"

"Ah…well, not exactly. I kind of didn't call her."

A quick smile spread across Zia's face.

"I was thinking maybe you could come over to my apartment after dinner. You know…full moon…universe."

Selene blushed. "Hmm, good idea."

They crossed at the light and suddenly Selene halted and put her arm in front of Zia to stop him…then, turned to him.

"Zia, I just remembered something. The night I found out you were Dad's son, I was hysterical, and after I ran to get my car in front of Boyd's, I drove around and around and when I was coming down 66 by that bar just ahead of us, I saw Jerry coming out with a guy."

"So," Zia shrugged.

"Zia, it's a bar where homosexuals hang out—everyone knows that. What was Jerry doing there?"

"I don't know Selene. Jerry never talks about where he goes or what he does. He might say he's stopping for a drink or a beer, but that's it. That's why they call it a person's *private* life."

Selene took a deep breath as they stepped along closer to the bar, noticing that the door halfway open, she peered in. Jerry sat face to face with a guy at the bar oblivious to Selene's stare.

She ran a few steps to catch up to Zia and grabbed his arm.

"He's in there." She put her hands together like she was about to pray—inches apart. "This close to another guy."

"Calm down, Selene. That is none of our business. Let's go to dinner."

"Well, if he's still there on our way back, I'm going to make you take a look inside, then you can tell me what you think."

They enjoyed a delicious Italian meal, but Selene confessed that she was glad she wasn't Italian.

"Okay, Miss Chile Pepper, let's walk to our cars, and you can follow me to my apartment."

A ruckus ahead of them got their attention.

"Someone is beating up a guy down the street, Zia. I swear, it's

Jerry. Hurry. Hurry."

They ran to find Jerry lying slumped on the sidewalk and his attacker running down 66.

"Selene, stay with Jerry and have someone call an ambulance and the police. I'll try to catch the guy."

Zia sped after the muscular attacker, and yelled for help in Navajo to a group gathered near the corner. The Navajos quickly grabbed the guy. Zia got there almost instantly and helped them lead him back to the scene of his assault on Jerry. The attacker reeked of alcohol.

Sirens screeched.

"Why did you beat him up?" Zia asked.

"Because, he came out of that bar—that means he's a queer, a homo, a faggot!" He spat on the sidewalk.

Zia gripped the attacker's arm tighter and pulled him to where a crowd had gathered around Jerry. Selene wiped blood from Jerry's face with a wet towel from the bar, as he sat dazed.

Sirens, flashing lights, police cars and an ambulance added confusion.

"Officer," Zia said. "I'm a witness, and this is the guy who attacked our co-worker."

"Can you identify this man as your assailant?" the policeman asked Jerry.

Jerry looked up at him and nodded, "Yes."

The officer turned to where Zia and the other Navajos held onto the drunken assailant.

"Okay, you're under arrest." He turned to a fellow officer, "Cuff this guy and take him in."

"We'll get your statement later," the officer leaned over and told Jerry. "The ambulance is here for you now."

Selene motioned to Zia, and he walked over next to where she knelt with Jerry.

"Zia, I think we need to be at the hospital with Jerry. I'll ride in the ambulance, if you'll meet me over there."

"Sure."

After the paramedics loaded Jerry onto a stretcher and pushed him into the ambulance, he watched Selene hop into the front seat with the driver. Then he jogged to his car and headed for the emergency room.

My life is a magnet for bad luck, Zia thought. Every time I think I'm getting closer to Selene, a coyote—real or imaginary—crosses my path.

Selene paced the emergency waiting room while a doctor examined Jerry. Soon Zia raced in. "Any news?"

"Not yet. I just can't understand why someone would attack Jerry."

Selene rubbed her forehead.

"It didn't matter who it was, Selene. That drunk planned to beat up the next person who walked out of that bar."

They sat and drank hospital coffee and waited...waited. Finally, a nurse came through the double doors and motioned for them.

"You can see Mr. Davis now," she said as they followed her into the emergency room. "We're keeping him overnight to observe him for head injuries, so we'll move him to a room soon. He's going to be okay. He has a couple of broken ribs and is bruised up. We put some stitches in his forehead, and it looks like he's going to have a nasty black eye."

They passed several beds where curtains were drawn, then the nurse stopped and as she opened the curtain turned and said, "Now we've given him a sedative, so he might seem a little groggy. And remember, no smoking for him."

Selene walked over and touched the bed railing and whispered, "Hi, Jerry…you okay?"

"I guess," and he looked away.

Zia stepped up beside Selene. "Jerry, the nurse said you're going to be fine."

"Fine. Fine. Sure. I'll never be fine. Now that you know what I really am, I'll be out of this dump of a town as soon as I can." He turned his head away from them.

"Relax, Jerry," Zia said. "We don't hold anything against you. If you really want to leave town, you can. But don't feel like you have to."

Zia stepped around the bed to where he could talk to Jerry face to face and spoke softly.

"Jerry, I want to tell you how I was taught growing up Navajo. The *Nadleeh,* as you are called in the Navajo Way, have always been an essential part of our Navajo way of life. The Two-Spirit people exist in our ancient traditions, our creation stories, our ceremonies and songs."

Jerry said nothing, but sunk into his pillow.

A tear dropped onto Selene's cheek. "Zia, I never knew that."

"Your dad was raised around old Navajo traditions. Has he ever shown any discrimination against the Nadleeh?"

"Never. Then why is it this way…now?" she said looking toward Jerry.

Jerry scooted up in the bed and winced. "It's mostly Christians."

"I agree," Zia said. "The culture of the Western world fuels discrimination—even some Navajos don't respect the Nadleeh anymore."

"Can it ever change?" Selene asked.

Zia paced. "I don't know. Maybe the Nadleeh have to come out of hiding."

"I guess we can't all live in San Francisco," Jerry sighed. "At least Nadleeh sounds better than faggot and queer." Weary, he fell back against the pillow.

"Well, Jerry, right now you look more like a guy who just lost a prize fight," Zia laughed.

Jerry lowered his eyes.

"Yeah, and I feel like it, too." He turned to them and said, "Thanks for being here. I mean it."

The nurse breezed through with an announcement that Jerry would be moved to a room. "The police will be here to interview you. They would like you two to stay," she said pointing to Zia and Selene. "You're witnesses. Sorry you have to wait so long…it's Saturday night in Gallup." She shrugged her shoulders and left.

Well, another coyote just crossed my path, Zia thought. This could take all night.

"We're moving Mr. Davis to room 242," the nurse said. "Transportation will be here in a few minutes. Once we get him there, we have to do a history and physical, get him in a gown, so you two might want to go to the cafeteria and have a cup of coffee. If the police arrive, we can page you. Otherwise, give us about thirty minutes."

They walked down the long hallway to the cafeteria—dimly lit and closed down except for the free coffee station. A few people sat at tables sipping coffee and talking softly.

They each poured coffee into styro-foam cups and grabbed a few packages of sugar and powdered cream and headed for a table in the corner.

"It looks like this could be a long night, Zia."

Selene lifted her cup in a toast. "To what could have been."

"Yes," he sighed. "Here we sit."

"Actually, Selene, there are some things we need to talk about."

"Like what?"

Zia leaned forward, pushing his coffee aside.

"You saw the big suitcase and the canvas bag in the vault, didn't you?"

She nodded.

"Ben wants us to do something with the money—put it in the bank, invest it...something."

Selene ran her fingers through her hair and pulled it back as if she

225

were putting in a ponytail.

"Zia, I hate to admit it, but I've thought about what I'd like to do with some of that money. First, I think I should pay my own tuition. That's only fair."

"Sure, that makes sense to me."

Selene leaned forward, her eyes widened with excitement.

"Listen to this! Yesterday, Dr. Ortiz showed me a program where I could study in Spain. She said that would improve my Spanish and give me more credibility as an *international* journalist. It sounds so exciting, and it would take some investment to pull it off. What do you think?"

It felt like a gut punch to Zia—another coyote crossing his path.

"You're awfully quiet. What do you think?"

"Well, Selene…it's…you know…a…I think it's a fantastic opportunity for you."

She leaned back in her chair and folded her arms.

"What do *you* want to do with *your* money?"

Zia put his hands around the coffee cup and swirled the last of the brew around the bottom.

"For me, it's all about the Academy. I'd like to see it happen. It's going to take a lot more money than what I'll have, but…but at least it's a start…a commitment."

"What if you used some of it to go on and get your Master's, Zia?"

He shook his head.

"No, as far as I'm concerned, I'm getting my Master's right now. I don't need to prolong the agony. I want to get started."

Selene unfolded her arms and slapped one hand on the table and burst into laughter.

"That sounds so Ben Monroe-ish! Can't you see it…you're the one who grew up to be like him…not me."

"You know something, Selene, these last few months have changed my life. You just made me realize that…maybe for you…going to Spain might create some interesting developments."

"You're right, Zia. I guess I've been overprotected and pampered. I suppose I have some serious self-discovery to encounter. I wonder how Spain would change me."

The load speaker hissed. "Would Zia Yazzie and Selene Monroe please report to room 242."

"Okay, here goes mutton," Zia said in his Navajo accent.

By the time the police interview was over and they left the hospital, it was close to sunrise. Zia suggested stopping at an all-night pancake house and having breakfast.

"After we eat, I'll call Luz from the phone booth. She'll already be up saying her rosary. I don't want to zip in the back door and scare the hell out of her."

"Okay, then I'll drop you off at your car and see you back at the store for opening. It's going to be a long day."

***

A bit of sunlight slid through the drapes as Cecelia slipped out of bed and opened them enough to scan the undulating hills of Tesuque, graced with tall juniper and piñon, and dotted with squat rabbit brush. She wondered who lived in the secluded, sprawling homes tucked away in the landscape. Cecelia was careful not to wake Ben—surely exhausted from their night of lovemaking. She longed to step out onto the balcony and inhale the crisp morning air, but her teddy was too revealing.

"Come back to bed, Cecelia. I don't want our honeymoon to be over so soon."

"Yes, dear. It's been the best honeymoon ever. We're in no hurry."

She closed the drapes.

It was nearly mid-morning before they emerged from their room.

"I think champagne and eggs Benedict are warranted after that performance. How about you, Cecelia?"

"Absolutely," she grinned.

I'll never look at another woman again, he thought.

They held hands and walked toward the restaurant.

"You know something?" Ben stopped in his tracks. "I...I actually forgot about the store."

Cecelia leaned into his chest. "That's shocking," she chuckled. "But it seems that reality is creeping back, isn't it?"

"You're right. Let's eat and then head home. God only knows what's going on."

"Oh relax," Cecelia said, "It's just a quiet Sunday."

***

Zia stopped by the hospital before he opened the store. A long hot shower helped to revive him, but he felt groggy. Room 242 buzzed with activity. Jerry was scheduled for a chest x-ray, blood work and other tests to verify he was healthy enough to go home. The doctor would be in to see him and complete discharge instructions and write necessary prescriptions as soon as all testing was complete.

"Jerry, call the store when they're about to release you, so I can pick you up and take you home. We can get your car and anything else you need after we close the store.

"Okay, will do."

"See you later, then."

Selene arrived at the store on schedule, and Zia admired how she could look so fresh and beautiful without any sleep.

"Good morning, Zia, long time no look."

Zia told her the plans to pick up Jerry and get his car later.

"Gee, maybe I should pick him up. You don't want to leave me here in the store alone when I've only had one day of training."

"That's true. Well, let's get started. I'll open the vault then you can get the cash drawer set up."

"Okay, neatly—all the bills straightened and facing the same direction. No folded edges. Got it."

With the opening duties done, Zia asked Selene to step into the vault. "Can you stay over another day so we can take this money to the bank?"

"As long as I leave by mid-morning to get to class on time."

"Ben is good friends with the president of the bank. Maybe he can call him at home and arrange to meet us there before they open to deposit this cash. If we walked in during business hours, they'd think we were drug dealers."

Selene laughed. "For sure," she pointed to the stash. "This looks like drug money from the '50s."

Zia strolled through the store inspecting showcases and inventory. He wanted everything well-stocked and in order before Ben and Cecelia returned.

"Selene, can you straighten these earring trays and add new merchandise from back stock in the vault?"

"You've got it, boss."

"If you don't mind…before we get busy…I'm going to sit in the office and work on my school project. This section is due on Thursday."

"Sure, no problem."

Selene stocked and straightened earrings then memorized where things went in the showcases and studied the merchandise. She sprayed glass cleaner and wiped fingerprints from the showcases and moved about the store. She knew if she sat down and studied the various turquoise mines in the book Zia gave her yesterday, she would fall asleep.

Later, Zia stepped out of the office and paced near the vault.

"Selene, there's something else I need to talk to you about…for the Academy."

"Okay, what's your latest idea?"

"I'm working on the business plan for my presentation this week. It details cost, budget… location." He shoved his hands in his pockets.

"So, here goes…I'd like to use our five acres in Thoreau and the old store building as the initial location for the Academy. But, half of it is yours, and I need your approval."

"Absolutely. Do it!"

"This is business, Selene. Do you want to be a partner? Do you want me to buy you out? Do you want to be involved in ownership and let your investment grow…or fail? I just don't know how to approach it."

"I don't know either. This is probably something Dad could advise us on. For the sake of your presentation, you should go ahead as if you are the sole owner. You're being too honorable again. That committee is interested in the concept, not the ownership."

Zia paced. "You're right, Selene. I was complicating it too much."

Selene moved toward him and took his hands in hers and looked him in the eyes. "Zia, this is your dream. The fact that you own a five-acre parcel to begin your Academy is going to knock the socks off the panel. The dean might croak instead of making a mockery out of you."

An inspired smile spread over Zia's face. "Well, you made my day. Now, if you don't mind, I'll sit in the office a while and let my imagination run wild."

"And I'll try to stay awake," Selene assured him.

Selene worked with customers while Zia mapped out the campus

231

for his proposed Academy. He felt relaxed and comfortable having her in the store.

The phone rang, and Zia answered in the office. Selene opened the office door and listened to Zia talk to Jerry.

"Sure, Jerry. That's nice...of course. Do what the doctor said, and don't worry about work until you're up to it. I'll talk to Ben about your commission check. Take care. Oh, you're welcome."

"What's up?"

Zia turned in the chair to face Selene.

"His friend is picking him up at the hospital and taking him home. Jerry said his friend will get the prescriptions and buy him some groceries, and he'll get another guy they know to bring the car back to his trailer. You heard the rest."

"Sounds good. Speaking of sounds, my stomach is growling."

"Surprise, surprise, Selene."

Zia gave her some cash to pick up sandwiches.

"Get whatever you want, Selene, but please no more coffee. I can't take it."

The day seemed to stretch on forever, and while Zia was supervising Selene checking out the drawer at closing, Ben and Cecelia walked in—all smiles.

"You two look exhausted. Was it that busy today?" Ben asked.

"No," Zia answered.

"There's so much to tell you, Ben. Can we sit down somewhere and talk?"

"Why don't we all go to dinner and relax and catch up on

everything," Cecelia suggested.

"Good idea."

***

When Louise unlocked the store Monday morning, she heard their voices in the vault—Zia, Ben, Cecelia and Selene.

"This cash of yours has bothered me for a while now. It's a problem. I don't know how much money there is, and we can't walk into the bank without creating some serious questions. I don't care if the bank president is my friend, he's going to wonder. This is money that should have been declared, reported, taxed. I don't want to stir up controversy."

"I understand," Zia said.

"Me too, Dad. I get the problem it will cause."

"So here's my solution. I'll give each of you a check for a specific amount. I always need cash to buy jewelry. You can deposit your checks—no questions asked. I'll have my accountant figure out the proper way to handle everything. We'll just keep doing that until all the cash is gone. Or you can each take cash to have on hand. Let's ask Louise how much there is?"

Ben walked into the office to talk to Louise. Soon he motioned for the others to join him.

Louise pulled out a file folder that contained a series of adding machine tapes stapled together. The total was more than they expected.

Selene and Zia looked stunned.

"Louise, give them each a thousand cash and write them each checks for $10,000 to start. Just keep track of everything."

"I'll take care of it right now. I know Selene has to leave for Albuquerque."

When she finished, writing the checks and giving each of the cash, Zia counted out $20,000 from the suitcase while Ben prepared Louise for the news about Jerry.

"I've never been around homosexual people," she said. "I guess that's why he's so secretive and bigoted...he's probably been discriminated against himself.

Nobody else noticed that Selene had coaxed Cecelia away to the other side of the store where they each sat on a stack of Navajo rugs.

"Mom, so much has been going on that I didn't get to tell you that I saw David Stanfield when Zia and I were having lunch. He asked me a lot of questions and wanted to talk to you. He gave me his card."

She pulled the card from her purse and handed it to Cecelia.

"I don't want to have that conversation, but I guess I owe it to him."

"He already knows, Mom. Zia made me go to his office and tell him the truth. Then he told me that the first day we met, he noticed that my voice and other mannerisms were like his mother's and it jarred him so much, he had to leave."

Cecelia slumped in guilt.

"Don't do it to yourself, Mom. It's over. He's okay, and I'm okay with him. Now he wants me to meet his mother. Did you know her?"

"I met her once. She was a bit formal and aloof, but a lovely lady."

"Do you see anything of her in me?"

Cecelia stared at Selene. "I've never considered the possibility, Selene. I'm sorry. Maybe I was so locked up in my delusions I wouldn't allow it."

"So, are you going to call him?"

"Maybe, if I get my courage up."

Selene hopped up off the rugs. "I've got to go."

She walked toward her dad and Zia to say goodbye.

Zia stepped toward her and stopped.

"Selene, there are a couple of things I need to ask you. First, what if you and I each gave Jerry $500 from the stash to help him out?"

"Sure, that's kind of you to think that way—so Monroe-ish."

Zia rolled his eyes.

"What else, Zia?"

"Well, the other thing is that my cousin is having her *Kinaalda* next weekend, and I'd like you to go with me. It's her coming-of-age ceremony and it starts on Saturday evening and goes all night and finishes after sunrise on Sunday."

"Ay Dios, another all-nighter."

Zia laughed. "These events seem to be the only kind of all-nighters *we* get".

Selene put her index finger to her lip. "Sh."

"Anyway, Ben said it would be a good experience for you as part of your understanding of Navajo culture. I think so, too."

"It sounds fascinating. I'll be here."

Selene looked at her watch and gasped. "I have to leave now or drive 80 mph to get to my class on time."

"Goodbye, everyone," she yelled as she ran out the door. Then she turned. "See you Thursday, Zia."

While she waited for customers, Cecelia busied herself comparing photos and descriptions of turquoise from different mines to the stones in various pieces of jewelry. She'd pull something out of the showcase to identify the mine—then set it aside.

Ben brushed by her and squeezed her shoulder. "There'll be a test on that later."

He walked toward the vault lighting a cigarette.

"Zia, when Louise finishes the deposits, I'll go to the bank then drop by Jerry's house and give him the money from you and Selene. I need to reassure him that he has a job if he wants it. "

Zia raised his hand as if to ask a question.

"Ben, do you have a minute to talk about my project. I need your advice."

"Sure, son, what is it?"

He called me "son," Zia thought.

"It's an idea I've had for a while, and I talked it over with Selene already."

Zia detailed the plan as Ben sat on a stool at the work table in the vault. He gave him various scenarios.

"I like it! The thought of using that property honors my parents' memory, and it means that the money they stashed will benefit the people they came to love. You've got my mind racing, Zia."

Ben stood up and sucked in the last of his smoke and stubbed it out in the ash tray on the work table.

"Okay, I'm going to the bank and to Jerry's. When I get back, we can work here and draw it out. Unless you get busy…there's nothing pressing this morning…so you can work on your ideas while I'm gone."

Ben went into the office and picked up the deposit bag from Louise, turned and stopped short as he walked out the door. He leaned into the vault as he was about to leave.

"Zia, what if we redid the existing building and made *it* into the store that could support… and even promote the Academy's progress? I know you see the store as an important part of it—why not start it first?"

Zia snapped his fingers. "You're right. It would generate income, create awareness and help make the Academy a reality. Now you've got my mind racing, too."

Ben turned to leave the vault and stopped in short. "Zia, I don't want to interfere."

"No, Ben, you're not interfering. I'm asking for help."

***

The spring sunrise signaled the May winds to begin their fierce attack on the landscape. As Zia drove to Albuquerque, wind gusts pushed at his truck, debris blew across the highway, junipers twisted and dust devils swirled off the dry high desert. Every spring was the same. He remembered the searing sound and force of the winds at night as a child. It felt like it would surely lift their hogan and sail it through the air, like the story of Dorothy from Kansas in *The Wizard of Oz*—a book he'd read by flashlight as a youngster during a windy spring season.

Zia's project was ready and because it was so extensive, he had it copied at a local print shop and prepared four notebooks with specific sections separated by tabbed dividers. The presentation included a detailed Business Plan, a site plan of the Academy property with proposed buildings and usages, a drawing of the renovated retail store which included the merchandising plan and projected profit contributions to the future concept and a well-researched list of all possible tribal, federal and private grant possibilities.

He arrived early with the notebooks stacked in a shopping bag that read "Monroe Trading Company, Gallup, NM," and walked toward Dr. Ortiz's office.

"Good morning, Zia."

"Hello, Dr. Ortiz. I have my presentation prepared for everyone, so I'll leave this here with you and wait in the hallway until you're ready for me."

"My, this looks impressive."

"I can only hope," he said, thinking about the dean.

The group sat in the conference room perusing the presentation for nearly 20 minutes before Zia was invited to join them.

"Zia, this is completely out of the norm. Now suddenly you have five acres and a building—free and clear? Is this a work of fiction?" the dean demanded.

"No, sir. Let me explain. If you understand who I am, maybe it will help. First of all, I'm half Navajo and half White. I'm the illegitimate son of Ben Monroe, a well-known Indian trader in Gallup—a man who supported me, but, until recently, had never told anyone about me or my mother."

Zia registered the surprise they showed in their quiet reactions.

"I was raised by my mother in the Navajo Way, and my expectations were set in that world. I've always been interested in education for my people, but in the last several months everything changed for me."

Zia looked around the room and continued.

"A few months ago, my father insisted I move to Gallup to work in his business, because of this Indian jewelry boom. Oh, I was resentful. I only had one semester left to complete my degree. That's why, in order for me to graduate and still work, you created this independent study for me."

"Continue, Mr. Yazzie," the department chair said.

"But...suddenly I started learning new things. My dual worlds changed how I thought and how I developed my concepts."

He put his head down for a second.

"Then after all those years of thinking I was Navajo, I had the surprising realization about how many inherent traits I have from my father...and how they have influenced me."

He looked from one to the other.

"Now, for the part about the property and the building and the initial investment of cash: I inherited it from my grandparents—my father's parents. It came as a huge shock to me and felt undeserved. Finally, one day I stood there and stared at the land and the run-down building and the idea of starting the Academy there seemed natural—a blessing, if you will. So, as you see, the truth is stranger than fiction."

A thin smiled crossed the dean's face.

"Okay, let's hash this out Mr. Yazzie. I have to admit, business plans are not my area of expertise," the dean said.

After nearly an hour of going over every detail, the committee seemed satisfied with the plan.

The department chair said, "I'd like to make a suggestion. If you'll all agree, I think this portion of Mr. Yazzie's proposal more than satisfies the requirements for completion of his Independent Study."

"Oh, I agree," said Dr. Ortiz. "What more could he possibly do?"

"Actually, I agree, as well," said the dean looking over the top of his glasses. "So, Mr. Yazzie, it looks like you're going to graduate."

A look of pure surprise crossed Zia's face.

"Thank you, all of you…so much."

"Congratulations, Zia," Dr. Ortiz said proudly. We will complete and sign the necessary documents today and submit them for your graduation. So, get that cap and gown rented!"

Zia beamed. He couldn't stop a smile from spreading across his face. He thanked them again, picked up his notebook and raced to the Frontier to share his good news with Selene.

The dean stood up holding the notebook. "I'm going to present Zia's project at the Innovation Award meeting today. I haven't seen another submission that can compare."

He lifted his briefcase and set it on the conference table.

"I have every submission of his right here to show them," he said as he placed the notebook in his briefcase.

He looked from Dr. Ortiz to the department chair.

"Yes," he said, confidently. "I think we have our winner."

***

He scanned the restaurant and saw Selene seated at a corner table with David Stanfield.

"You're late, Zia."

"I have good reason. My presentation took longer, but the committee decided it satisfied the requirements for my Independent Study, and they're submitting the paperwork for my diploma as we speak," he said, elated. He set his notebook on the table and sank into a chair next to Selene.

"Wow, congratulations! That's fantastic. So, you're done with school while the rest of us still have to cram for finals."

"Yes, many good luckies for me," he said with his Navajo accent.

"Hello, David," Zia said, reaching out to shake his hand. "I didn't mean to ignore you...I was just so excited about everything."

"Congratulations, it sounds like you put in a lot of work into your project. Can I take a look at it?"

"Sure, this is the final segment," Zia nodded, and slid the

notebook across the table to David, then turned to Selene.

"So, while we were waiting for you, I started to tell David about our soap opera lives."

"It's quite a story, Zia," David said looking up from the proposal. "I'm glad it seems to be calming down to some sense of normalcy for you both…if you can call it that."

"I guess it has to seem *normal* to us," Zia chuckled. "We have no choice."

"Well, green chile burgers and fries on me to celebrate all the milestones we've conquered," David said.

They talked about Zia's project during lunch, and he told Selene to keep the notebook and bring it with her Saturday when she came to Gallup for his cousin's Kinaalda.

"Selene, you need to read this and give me your input."

Zia left quickly after lunch. He knew Selene needed to spend time with her father. Besides, he intended to stop by his mother's and give her the good news, and he couldn't wait to tell Ben—thanks to his help—this presentation was a grand slam. He would graduate.

After Zia left, David leaned forward and folded his hands.

"Selene, I told my mother about you, and at first she was shocked. The last few times I've talked to her, she's warming to the idea. She's coming for graduation and wants to meet you."

Selene gulped. "Okay, I guess that's not as dramatic as going to New York, although it makes me a little nervous."

"She'll love you. You'll get along great. Oh, are you going to be at graduation?"

"I'm sure I am now, with Zia graduating. That will be a big occasion."

"Good, because this year I'll be presenting the Innovation Award. My mother will be sitting up front with the family of the winner. She loves that stuff. It's possible I can get you a seat with her."

Selene immediately shook her head, no. "I have to sit with my family…Zia's family…uh, you know."

"Of course, I understand. We'll arrange to meet the following day for lunch then. How's that?"

"Yes, that would be nice."

David looked at his watch. "Oh, I have to go. I have a meeting with the dean in 15 minutes to select the winner of the Innovation Award."

He slipped the notebook across the table to Selene.

"This proposal of Zia's seems quite interesting. Can you tell me more about it another time?"

***

After they closed the store Saturday afternoon, Zia and Selene hopped in Zia's truck and drove east on Route 66 heading for I-40 and Thoreau, while Zia explained the coming-of-age ceremony.

"My cousin, Emma, is thirteen. The Kinaalda honors her womanhood and has to be performed within a month of her first moon. You know…her menstrual cycle."

Selene straightened.

"I learned that I couldn't be on *my moon* for our sweat bath...first time I ever heard it called that."

Zia looked over at Selene. "Hmm, look at all you've learned about Navajos."

"Funny."

"We're due there for the feast before the ceremony...that begins at dusk. My uncle will have butchered a sheep—slabs of mutton will be grilling, and cuts and ribs frying on the wood stove in their open-air summer hogan. Ah, I can smell it already. My aunts and my mother will be making fry bread. I'm getting hungry just thinking about it."

Zia shifted in his seat.

"The last four days of preparations have been tough for Emma. She's had to run long distances to condition herself. And, I can assure you, she has ground bushels of corn for the cake. It's one of the requirements, and it is hard work. Since most of our clan will be attending the ceremony, there has to be enough, and the cake is always a favorite."

"Wait, Zia. Tell me how they make this ground corn into a cake."

"Her mother and aunts make a batter of the ground corn, water, sugar and sometimes raisins. The uncles have already dug a large round, flat pit in the earth and...well, we'll be there to see the whole thing happen, so I don't want to spoil it now."

"I can't wait," Selene said.

"After the food feast, the ceremony begins at dusk and lasts all night. Everyone enters and sits on the floor against the log walls of the hogan while our clan Medicine Man performs the ritual sing. His songs are the prayers for Emma to become a good and strong woman."

"Fascinating, Zia."

Selene looked out toward the sandstone cliffs and the brilliant blue sky as they turned into Thoreau.

"Well, there's your future Academy, Zia."

"I hope so. Have you thought about your part in this, Selene?"

"Whatever I can do to help make it a success, I'll do—even if it's more from the suitcase fund. I just need enough money to pay my tuition and spend a semester or two in Spain."

"Allowing me to share your ownership in this property is more than enough," he said.

Selene rolled her window down. "Whatever you say...but the offer still holds. That's what families do, isn't it?"

That's it! The family thing, Zia thought. That's what's been bothering me.

Selene stuck her hand out the window to feel the air. "No wind. We're lucky."

"You better roll your up your window, we're headed up some dirt roads—it's a dusty climb."

Zia knew his way up the red dirt pathways—no road signs anywhere. Soon, they arrived at their destination at the base of the rugged sandstone cliffs.

Lots of pickup trucks were parked randomly in all directions, and Zia pulled in and parked under the high branches of a juniper tree.

Selene hopped out of the truck and grabbed her sweater and knotted it around her waist. She scanned the unfamiliar scene. Two hogans sat a short distance from one another. Looking to her left she saw what Zia had described as the open-air summer hogan where the mutton and fry bread were being prepared and where the feast would be held. The sheep were penned up nearby and dogs wandered lazily. The carcass of the newly-butchered sheep hung from a juniper tree.

"Selene," Zia interrupted her gaze. "Everyone is heading over to the spot where the cake will be baked. Come on."

"There's Emma with all of our aunts and my mother," Zia said, "Look across the way. They're standing in front of the cake pit ready to begin."

Emma was traditionally dressed in full-length green velveteen, her waist tied with a sash and cinched with a concho belt.

"She's wearing her mother's squash blossom necklace," Zia whispered.

"She looks beautiful." Selene turned to run to the truck. "Oh, I've got to get my camera."

Zia grabbed her arm to stop her.

"No cameras allowed, Selene."

"Oops. Sorry," Selene said.

The cake pit had darkened and solidified from the burning wood. The aunts carefully lined the pit with overlapping corn husks. They poured bowls of batter gently into the corn-husk lined pit. Next, they took turns and blessed the mix with powdery flecks of corn pollen—Emma did the same. Finally, the aunts covered the mix with a tightly woven fan of more corn husks. Then the men took over, covering everything with hot coals.

Selene leaned over and tugged on Zia's shirt. "I've never seen anything like this," she whispered.

"I know. The cake will bake slowly all night long. Family members take turns adding more hot coals as the night wears on," he said quietly. "We have to leave now. No one can stand and stare at the cake. That might ruin it. In the morning, they'll uncover it and everyone gets a nice warm piece of corn cake."

They followed the crowd of family back to the summer hogan for the feast. Long tables covered with red and white checked oil cloths held large platters of meat and fry bread and bowls of side dishes. Selene met many of Zia's family and gave Anjelah a quick hello as she busied herself at a cast-iron skillet making fry bread. As the meal ended, everyone entered the hogan clockwise and sat on the floor against the octagonal walls of the dwelling. Emma was seated near the wood stove with the Medicine Man. As the sun set, the hitaali's sing began.

Hours passed, and the hypnotic resonance of his Navajo chanting took Selene into a meditative state. Zia seemed to be in a faraway place, too.

At prescribed intervals, the Medicine Man passed his soft leather pouch of corn pollen around. Each guest took a small pinch of the pollen and placed it on their tongue, touched the top of their head, and then rubbed the residue off their fingers into the air toward Emma—as if blessing her.

Selene repeated what she witnessed when the pouch was passed to her. She felt honored to participate in the ritual and was empowered with new strength in her own womanhood and experienced a surge of independence. She thought about studying in Spain and the possibility of becoming a foreign correspondent. It all sounded so dreamy. But what about Zia?

Zia tapped Selene on the shoulder and whispered. "The main prayer is over, and it's okay to leave for a while. Let's get some fresh air and hot coffee."

Once outside, Selene said, "It's so hypnotic and mystical.

"Take some deep breaths, and we'll walk around a bit."

The night air held a chill, and Selene put her sweater on before they went to the summer hogan for coffee.

While they sat at a picnic table and drank coffee from styro-foam cups, Selene asked Zia to explain the significance of the corn pollen.

"Corn is a symbol of fertility and life for us." Zia said. He stood and slipped his hand in the pocket of his Wranglers and pulled out a small soft leather pouch and handed it to Selene. "This is my corn pollen. I always carry it with me. I use it as an offering every morning at dawn when I say my prayers to the Holy Deities."

Selene held the soft pouch as if it were some strange treasure. "There's so much I don't know about you," she said, handing him the pollen pouch.

"My pouch is nearly empty," he said. "In the summer, my mother and her sisters go to the cornfields and grasp the tassels of the corn to release the pollen into the bowls they bring with them. It's a sunny yellow dust, we call *tádídíín*, and they replenish our pouches," he said as he slipped his back into his pocket.

"Let's walk around a bit," Zia said.

Selene gazed up into a sphere of a zillion stars that seemed close enough to touch—and a full moon glowed. "Look, Zia, it's the universe. I've never experienced a night like this."

"You're away from city lights, and nothing can disturb the brilliance of the night sky, Moonbeam."

"Hello, universe, it's us," she called out… "Zia and Selene…we're still waiting."

They leaned back against a nearby pickup truck and gazed into the vast sparkling universe. Selene was convinced that every star and planet in existence was shining there for her to witness.

"Well, Zia, here we are face to face with the universe. So I guess it's time to figure *us* out."

"That's exactly what I was thinking about while I was meditating during the sing… and this is what the universe is telling me, Selene."

He moved away from the truck and stood in front of her.

"What if we…finally…get intimate? It changes everything. What if it doesn't work out, and we end up hating each other? I couldn't take that, Selene. You are so important to me, that I never want to lose you."

He took her hands in his and looked into her eyes.

"I know this sounds strange, but if you're my sister, I'll have you in my life forever. The love of a brother and sister is unconditional love."

Selene pulled her hands away from his, then leaned back and stared into the universe somewhat dazed. An uncomfortable silence drifted into the breeze that slipped past them.

Selene pushed herself away from the truck and paced the reservation earth and stopped to gaze into the brilliant night sky—as if looking for an answer.

She turned and walked back to where Zia stood with his head down, hands in his pockets, kicking the dirt with the tip of his cowboy boot.

"Zia, this is all so confusing. But maybe that's why the universe has kept us apart…ah, err…because our union is pure and platonic—and forever. I'm still not sure I understand or want to accept that. Maybe our relationship is unique to the universe, and we could have destroyed it. Think about…how many times…we almost…."

He took his hands out of his pockets, stepped toward her and held her hands in his again.

"I have, Selene…over and over. Tonight in the hogan I finally understood what has been gnawing away at me…that all along you were meant to be my sister."

She squeezed his hands in reassurance.

"Zia…you know, I've always wanted a brother, and you're the best one I could ever have," she sighed then put her head down and kicked a clod of dirt. "But, what if…what if when I come back Spain, I decide I don't want to be your sister anymore? Does the universe change?"

"Of course, the universe is ever-changing, Selene."

They stood side-by-side looking into the stars and put their arms around each other's waists.

"Selene, when you come back from Spain…you might be different…changed." He shrugged his shoulders. "But, we'll return to this very spot on a clear, star-filled night and see what the universe has in store for us then. We don't know yet. For now, we better go back into the hogan."

Selene took one last look into the heavens and winked. "Thanks for now, universe. What a night!" she sighed.

Back in the hogan, the hypnotic sing continued, and before dawn, two of Emma's aunts washed her hair with warm water and fresh yucca sap and arranged it with natural combs fashioned from yucca spines.

Then as the faint streak of light appeared on the horizon, Emma ran east out the hogan door to greet the rising sun.

Zia, Selene and many others, ran after her through the trees and shrub as the peach dawn burst forth from the horizon.

Then Emma sprinted back to the hogan door and outward again to complete her run in each of the four directions—Zia and Selene and the others jogged behind her on her final quest toward womanhood.

While everyone walked toward the unveiling of the corn cake, Zia and Selene stood together as sunrise captured the reservation sky. Zia slid the pollen pouch from his pocket, untied the soft leather lanyard and took a small portion of corn pollen between his thumb and forefinger—placed it on his tongue, then touched the top of his head

251

and offered the last flecks of pollen into the breeze toward sacred Turquoise Mountain. "Hozhó, to wisdom, harmony, knowledge and happiness."

He passed the pouch to Selene and she did the same. "To womanhood," she said, as she sprinkled the remaining specks of corn pollen into the break of day.

SYMBOL MEANINGS

A variety of symbols found in Navajo jewelry illustrate themes found in each Part of *The Turquoise Trader: A Zia Yazzie Novel*. While each Part of the book has a variety of story lines, the symbol chosen to represent a Part represents something within that narrative. The interpretation is sometimes right on, and sometimes loosely applied – the "possibility" of the symbolic meaning either by foreshadowing or a fate not meant to be.

New Mexico State Flag
The symbol on the New Mexico state flag is the image of the *Sun*. The main character in *The Turquoise Trader* is named Zia, which means "Sun". The Sun's rays represent Constancy. The Sun symbol is carried throughout the story, as this is, after all *A Zia Yazzie Novel*.

Part One: The Winds of Change
The central symbol here is *Rain*. While *Rain* means Prosperity, this is not actually a prosperous part of Zia's life, but one of prosperous possibilities. Rain also seems to signify the heaviness of the change occurring in Zia's life.

Part Two: Land of Enchantment
The *Big Mountain* symbol stands for Abundance.

Part Three: Dual Worlds Collide
The Navajo symbol used for this Part is *Paths Crossing*. Family members, friends, school mates all cross in worlds once thought to be separate, running along parallel but never intermingling paths.

Part Four: The Navajo Way

The Navajo, like many native tribes, referred to themselves as *"the people"*. In the Navajo language the word is *Diné*. The symbol used here stands for Human Life.

Part Five: The Whirling Log of Life

The symbol used here is the *Cloud*. While modern culture sees clouds as heavy or bringing darkness and rain, the Navajo interpretation of the *Cloud* is that of Prosperity. In this Part there is much that is "heavy," but lots of hopeful things occur also.

Part Six: Sterling Solutions

The Navajo symbol of the *Squash Blossom* stands for Courtship. Where will this rocky relationship lead?

ABOUT THE AUTHOR

Patricia Bezunartea consistently uses the southwest as the setting for her writing. She has spent her life in Arizona and New Mexico, where she and her late husband, Frank, developed businesses in Native American arts and crafts in the Phoenix area and later became the concessionaires at Bandelier National Monument, NM. Moving back to Arizona, they created a new southwest retail concept called "Peppers—the hottest little gifts shop in Scottsdale" and were featured in *Entrepreneur* magazine.

Patricia is a prize-winning author of many short stories. She has written the memoirs of Gilbert Ortega, nationally known Native American art dealer, as well as that of internationally known flamenco dancer, Lydia Torea.

She lives in Scottsdale and spends her summers in the Arizona high country where she researches and writes her novels. She is currently working on a medical-themed novel, as well as a sequel to her Zia Yazzie story.

Patricia is a member of the Scottsdale Society of Women Writers, Arizona Historical Novel Society and Arizona Authors Association.

www.ingramcontent.com/pod-product-compliance
Lightning Source LLC
Chambersburg PA
CBHW060909250626
47159CB00008B/2923